"Young readers will happily fall in line."
—Kirkus Reviews

"Frolicsome and breathlessly paced."
—Booklist

"Eye-grabbing black-and-pink graphics."
—Publishers Weekly

"The whole package is fresh and funny and even philosophical when it comes to values that third-graders understand."
—San Francisco Chronicle

Be sure to read **all** the **BABYMOUSE** books:

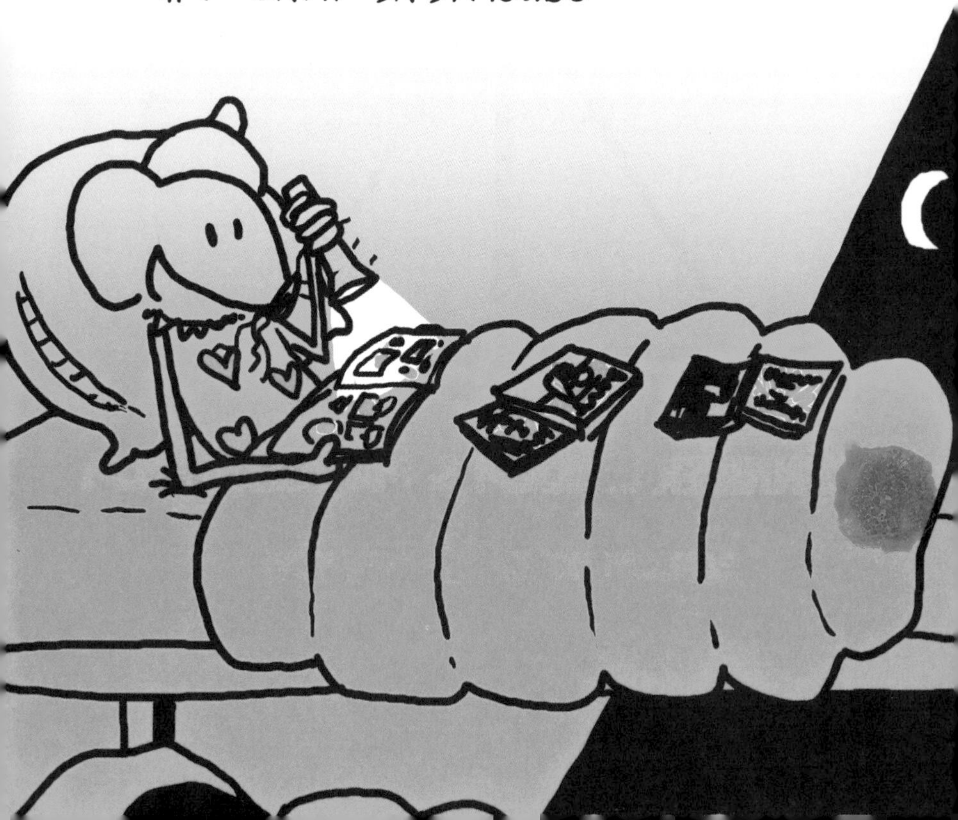

CAMP BABYMOUSE

BY JENNIFER L. HOLM & MATTHEW HOLM

RANDOM HOUSE NEW YORK

HEY! I'M **NOT** A WORK OF FICTION!

Copyright © 2007 by Jennifer Holm and Matthew Holm. All rights reserved. Published in the United States by Random House Children's Books, a division of Random House, Inc., New York.

www.randomhouse.com/kids
www.babymouse.com

Educators and librarians, for a variety of teaching tools, visit us at www.randomhouse.com/teachers

Library of Congress Cataloging-in-Publication Data
Holm, Jennifer L.
Babymouse : Camp Babymouse / Jennifer L. Holm and Matthew Holm.
   p. cm.
ISBN: 978-0-375-83988-7 (trade) — ISBN: 978-0-375-93988-4 (lib. bdg.)
I. Graphic novels. I. Holm, Matthew. II. Title. III. Title: Camp Babymouse.
PN6727.H592B26 2007   741.5—dc22   2006050391

PRINTED IN MALAYSIA 10 9 8 7 6 5 4 First Edition

RANDOM HOUSE and colophon are registered trademarks of Random House, Inc.

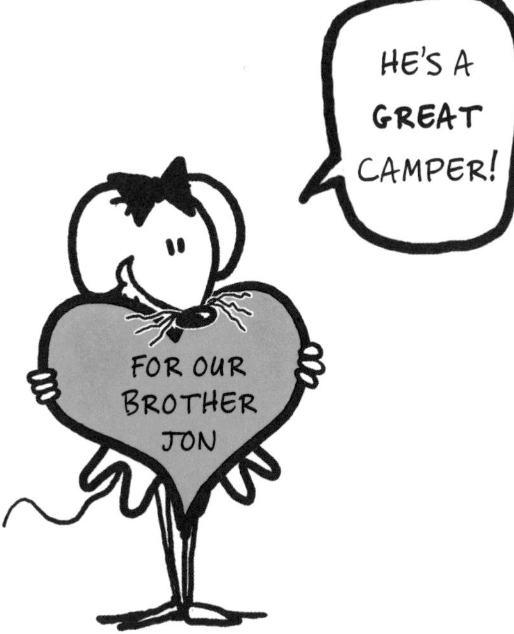
HE'S A **GREAT** CAMPER!
FOR OUR BROTHER JON

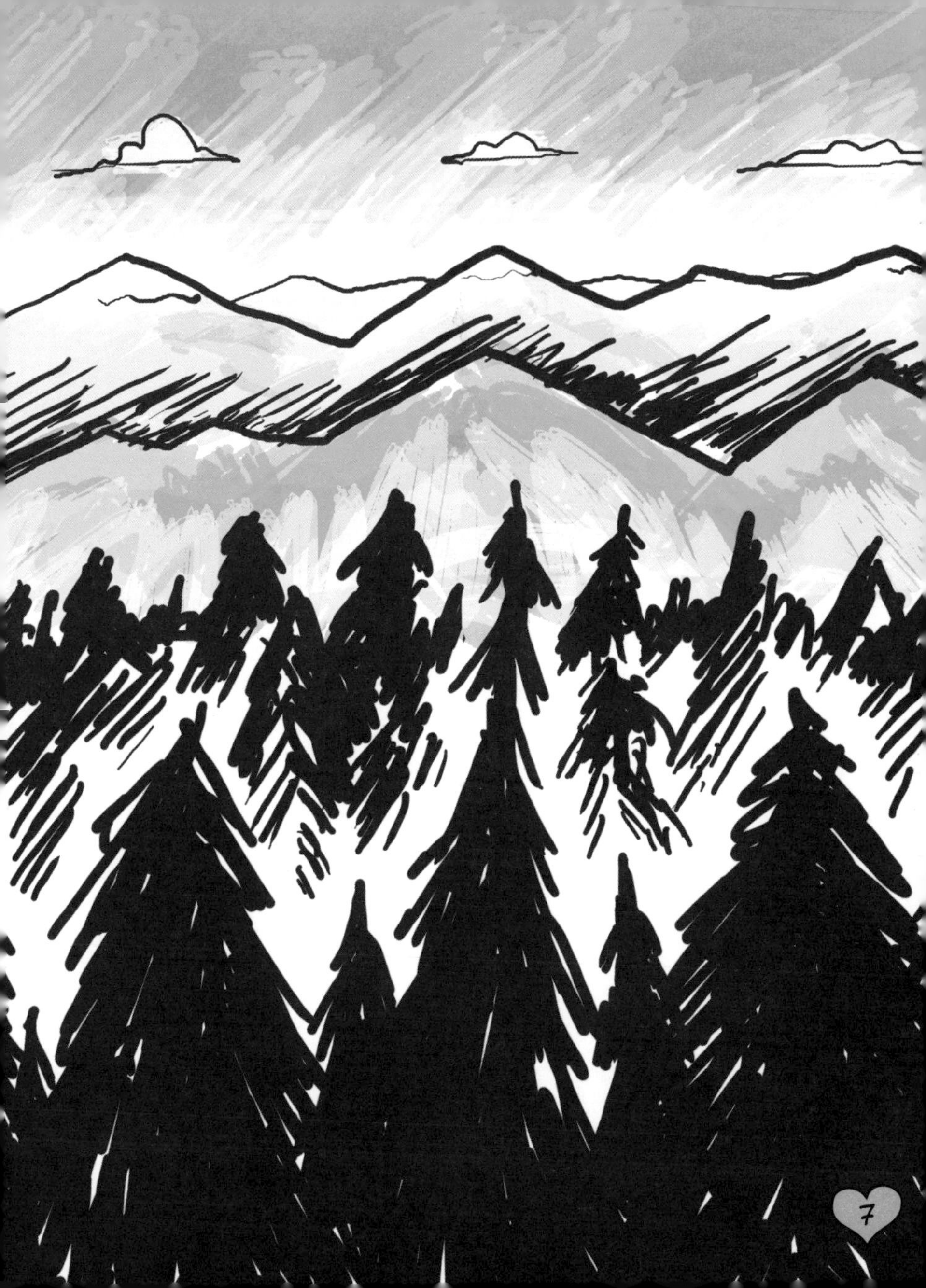

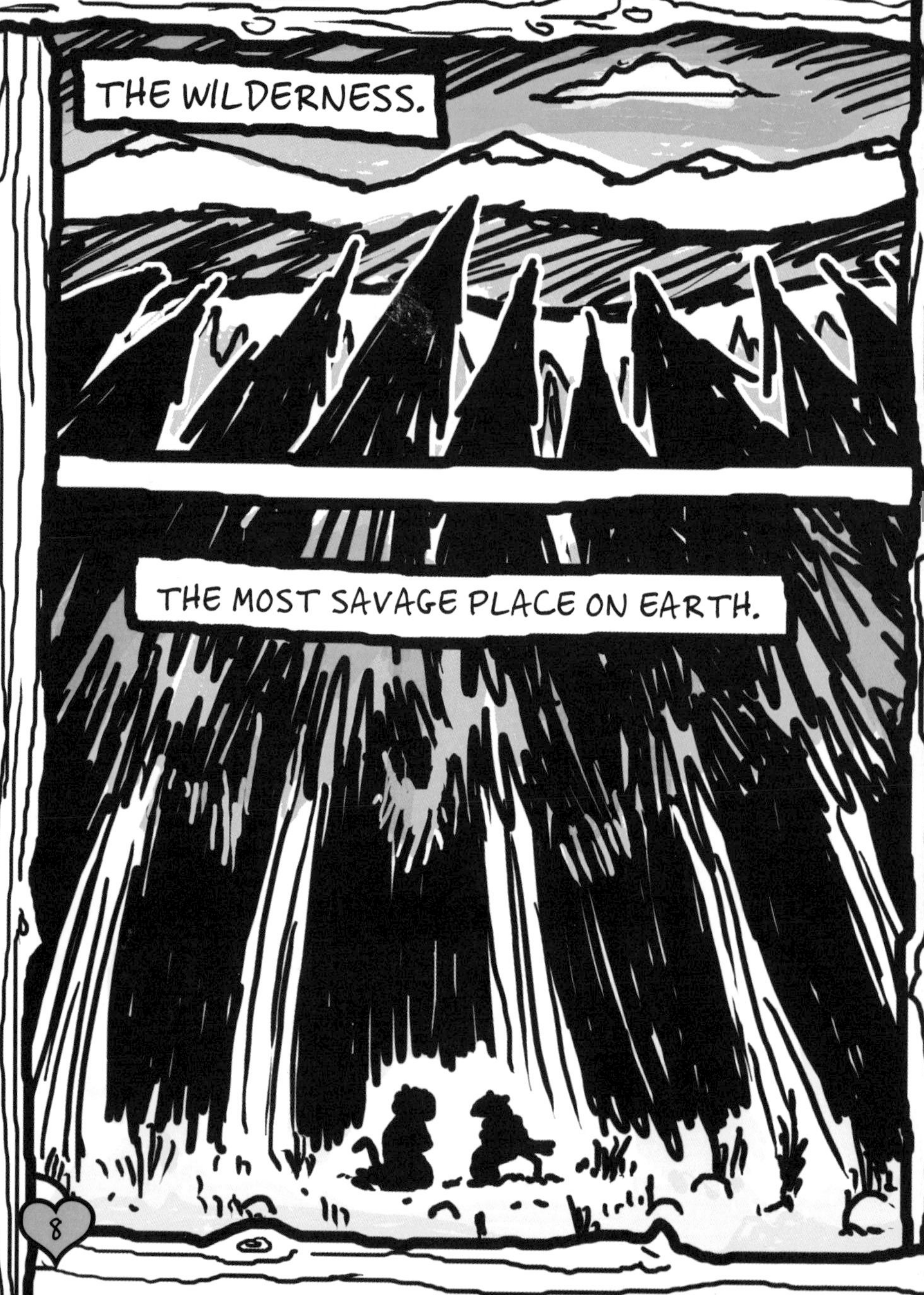
THE WILDERNESS.
THE MOST SAVAGE PLACE ON EARTH.

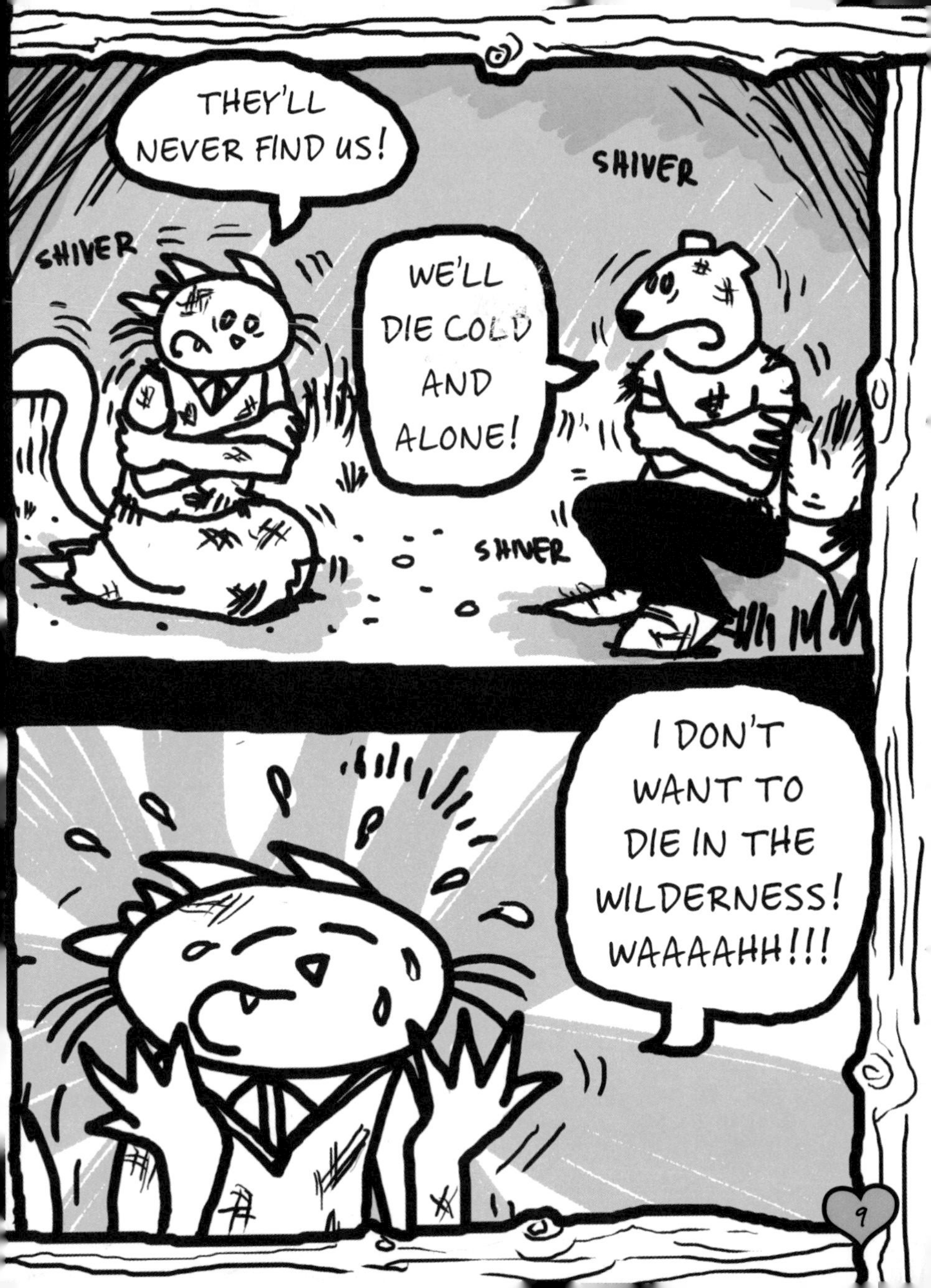
THEY'LL NEVER FIND US!
SHIVER
SHIVER
WE'LL DIE COLD AND ALONE!
SHIVER
I DON'T WANT TO DIE IN THE WILDERNESS! WAAAAHH!!!

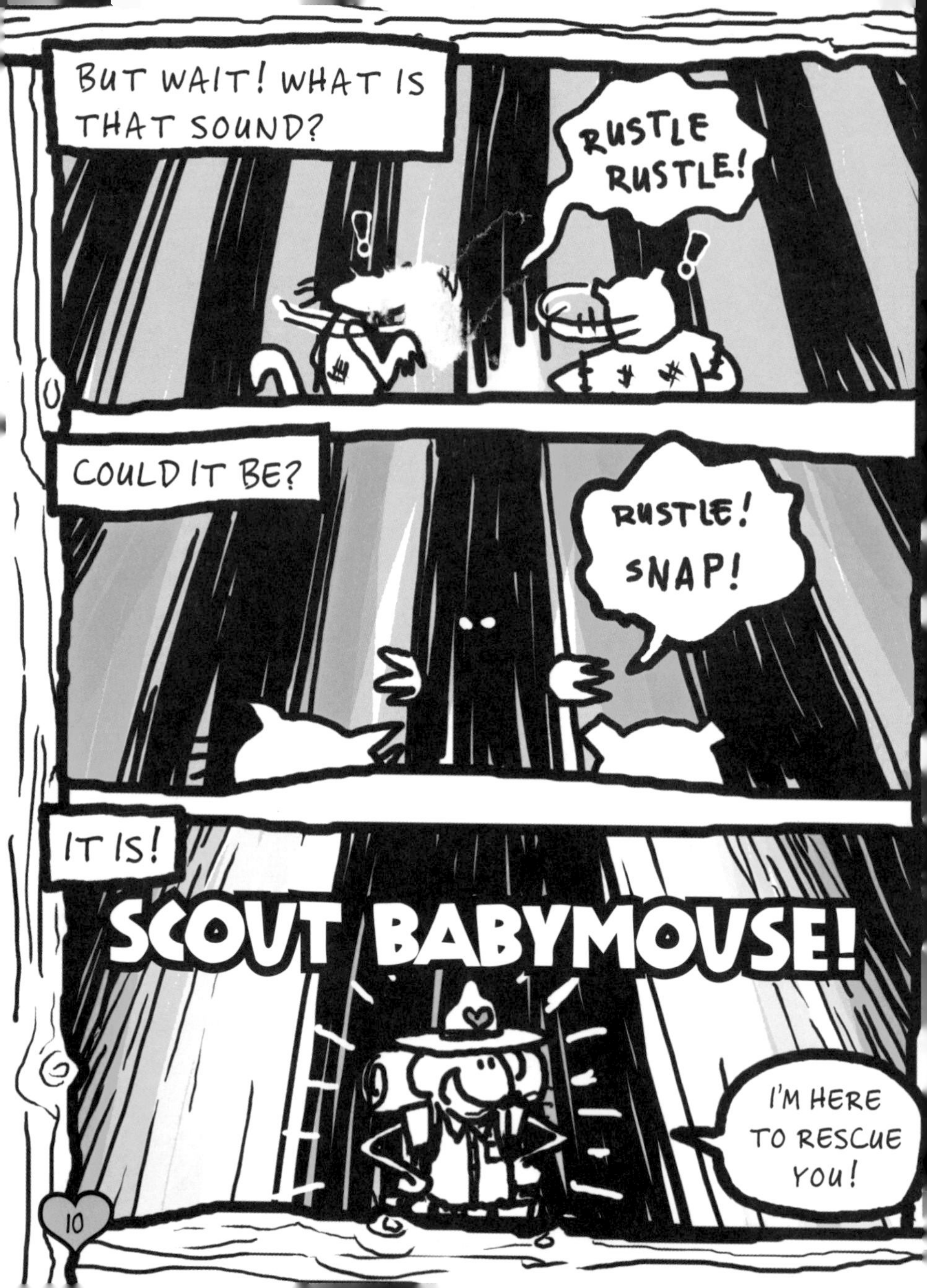
BUT WAIT! WHAT IS THAT SOUND?
RUSTLE RUSTLE!
COULD IT BE?
RUSTLE! SNAP!
IT IS!
SCOUT BABYMOUSE!
I'M HERE TO RESCUE YOU!

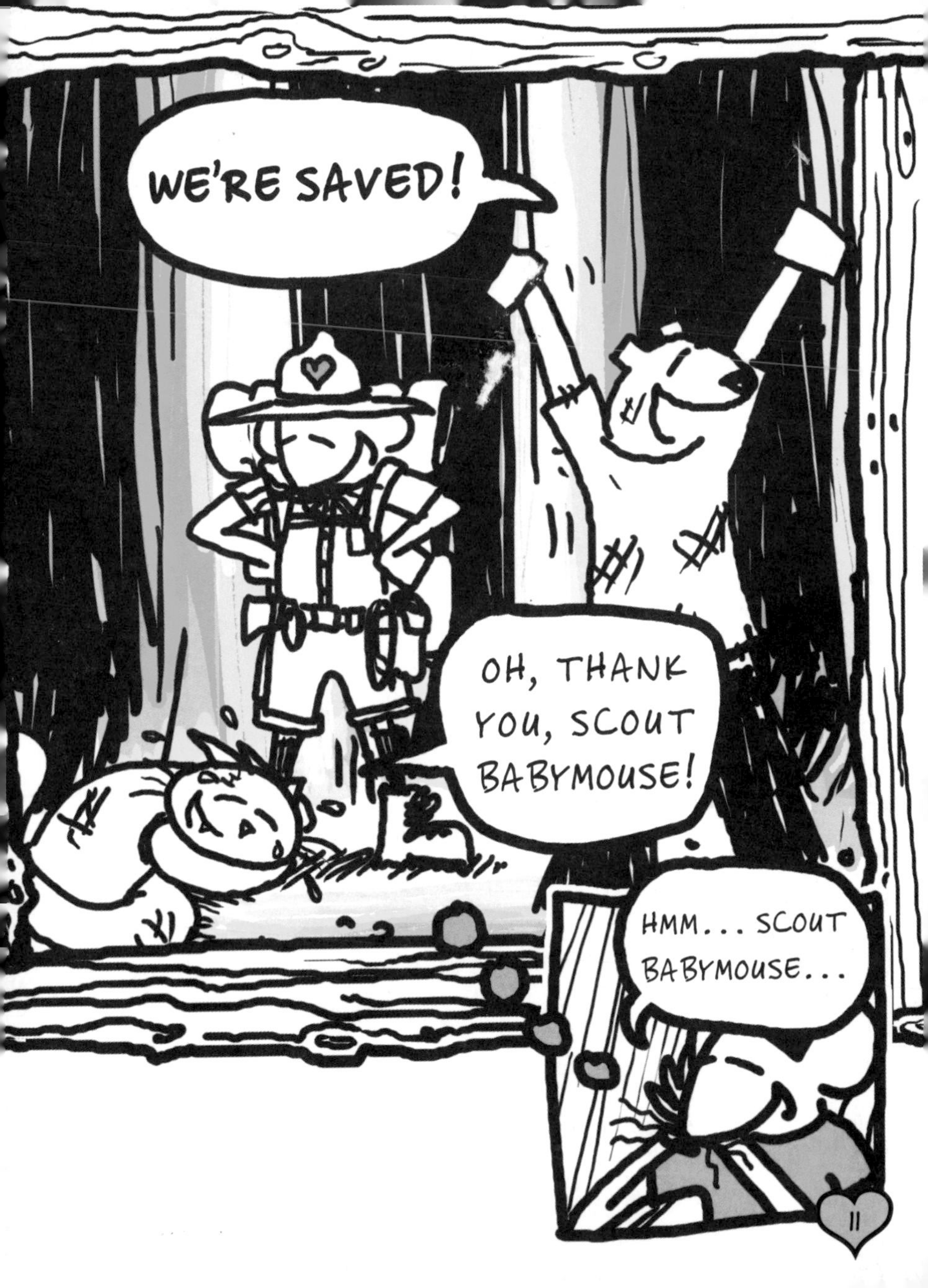
WE'RE SAVED!
OH, THANK YOU, SCOUT BABYMOUSE!
HMM... SCOUT BABYMOUSE...

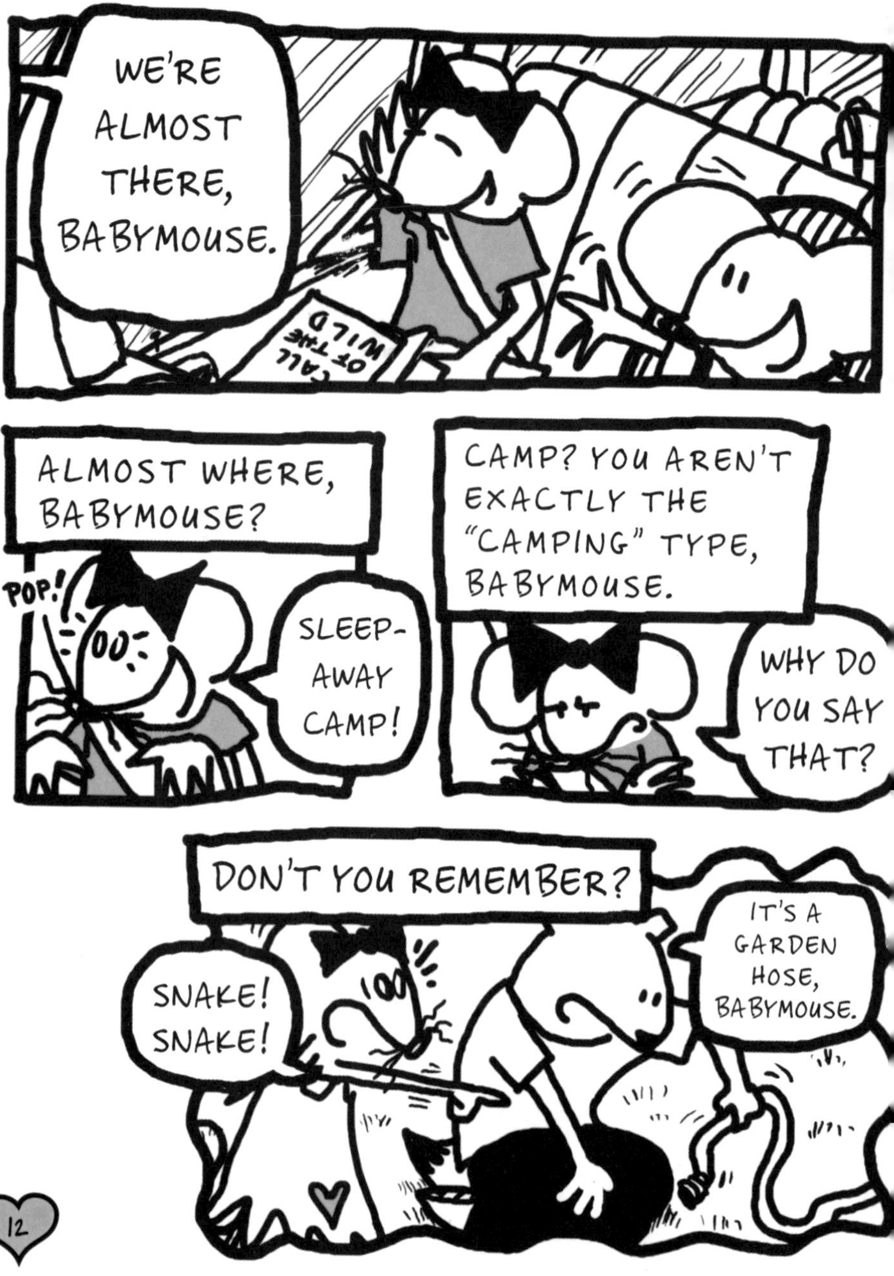
WE'RE ALMOST THERE, BABYMOUSE.
CALL OF THE WILD
ALMOST WHERE, BABYMOUSE?
POP!
SLEEP-AWAY CAMP!
CAMP? YOU AREN'T EXACTLY THE "CAMPING" TYPE, BABYMOUSE.
WHY DO YOU SAY THAT?
DON'T YOU REMEMBER?
SNAKE! SNAKE!
IT'S A GARDEN HOSE, BABYMOUSE.

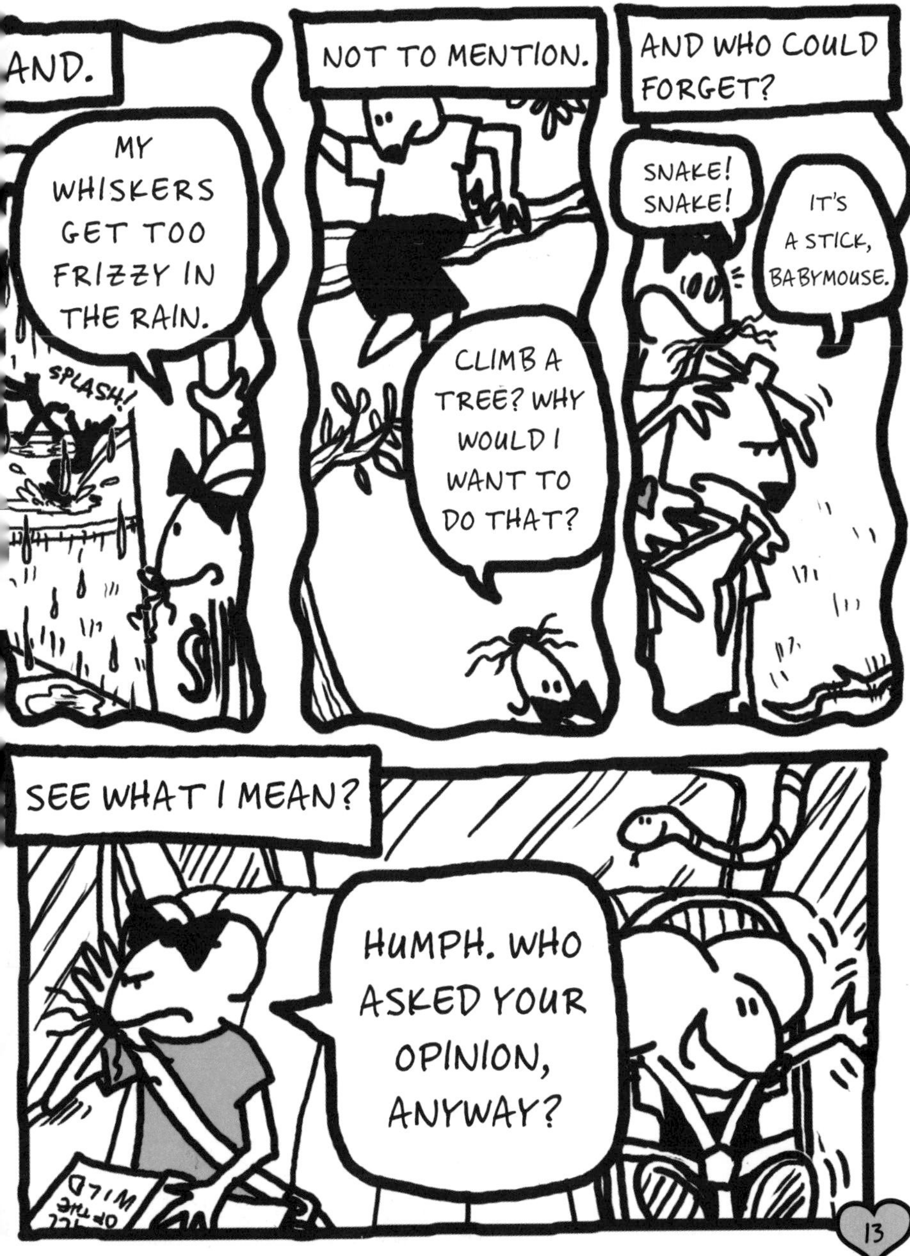
AND.
MY WHISKERS GET TOO FRIZZY IN THE RAIN.
SPLASH!
NOT TO MENTION.
CLIMB A TREE? WHY WOULD I WANT TO DO THAT?
AND WHO COULD FORGET?
SNAKE! SNAKE!
IT'S A STICK, BABYMOUSE.
SEE WHAT I MEAN?
HUMPH. WHO ASKED YOUR OPINION, ANYWAY?

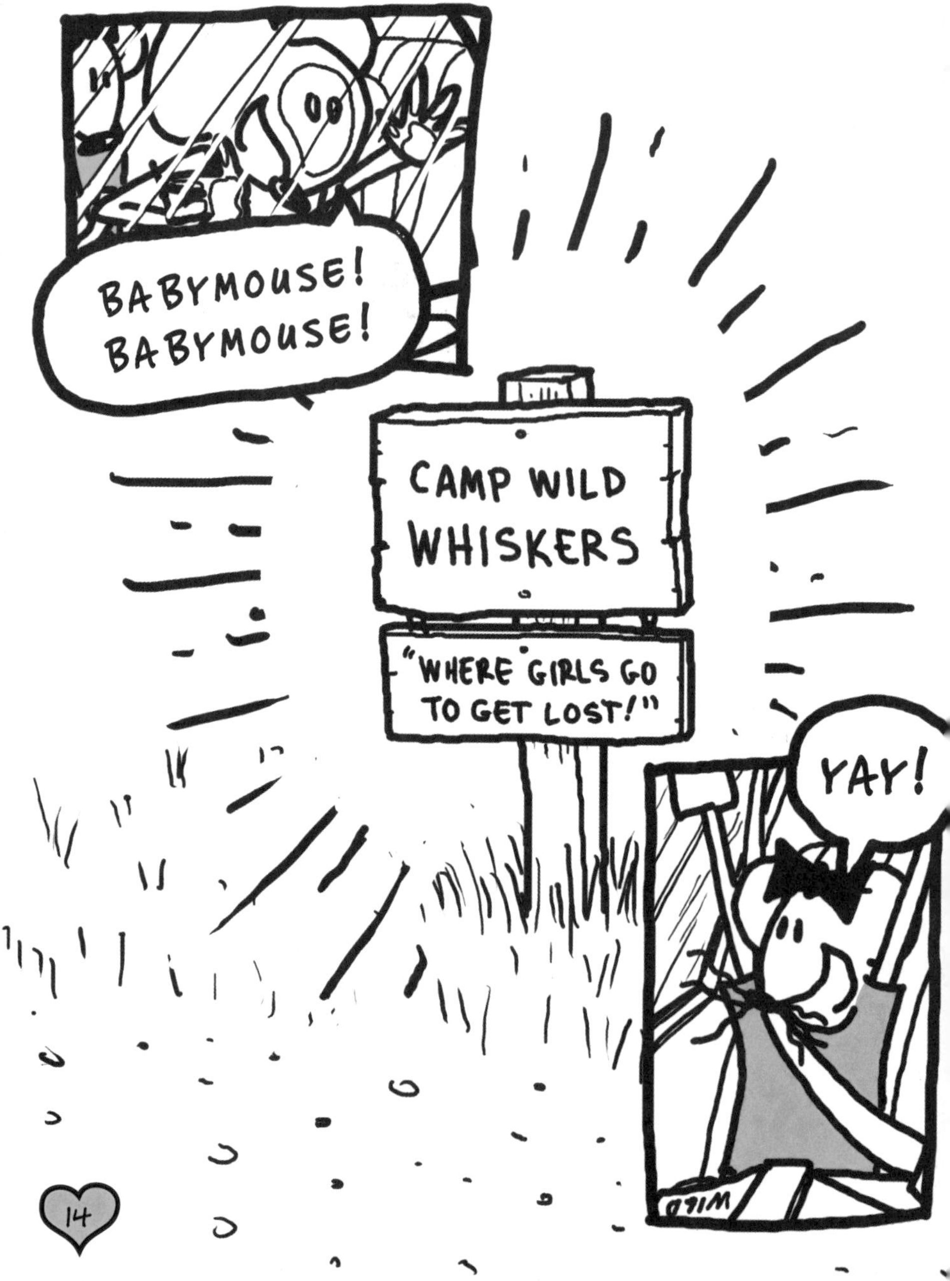
BABYMOUSE!
BABYMOUSE!
CAMP WILD
WHISKERS
"WHERE GIRLS GO
TO GET LOST!"
YAY!

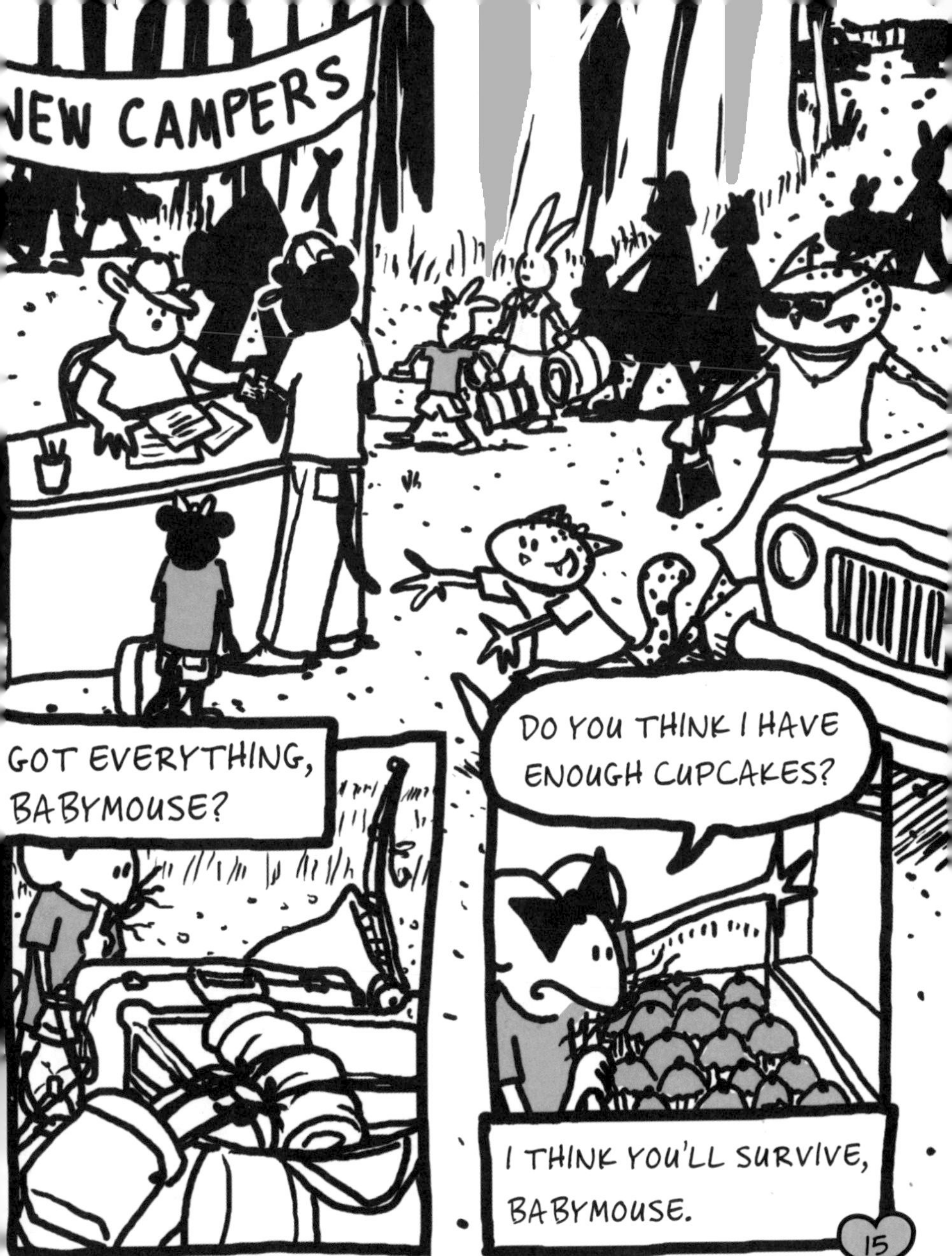

NEW CAMPERS
GOT EVERYTHING, BABYMOUSE?
DO YOU THINK I HAVE ENOUGH CUPCAKES?
I THINK YOU'LL SURVIVE, BABYMOUSE.

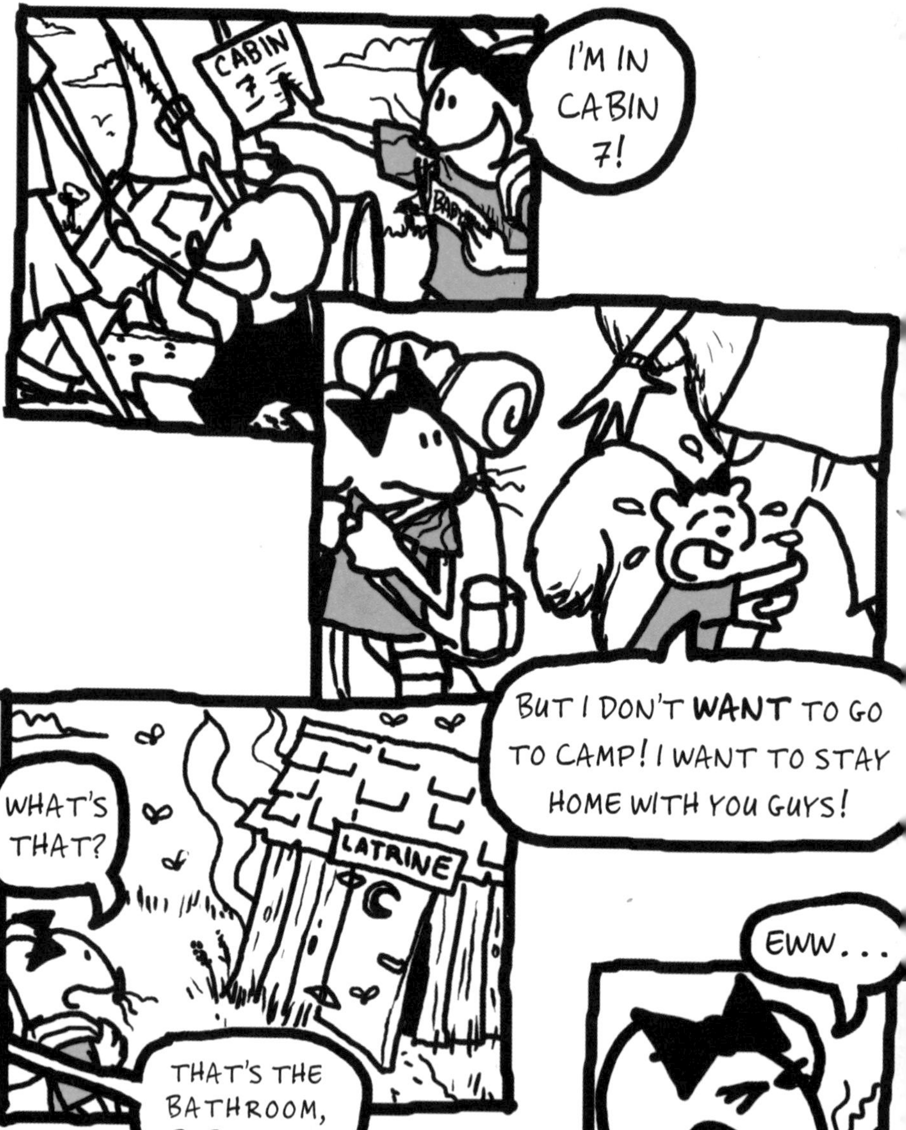
CABIN 7
I'M IN CABIN 7!
BUT I DON'T **WANT** TO GO TO CAMP! I WANT TO STAY HOME WITH YOU GUYS!
WHAT'S THAT?
LATRINE
THAT'S THE BATHROOM, BABYMOUSE.
EWW...

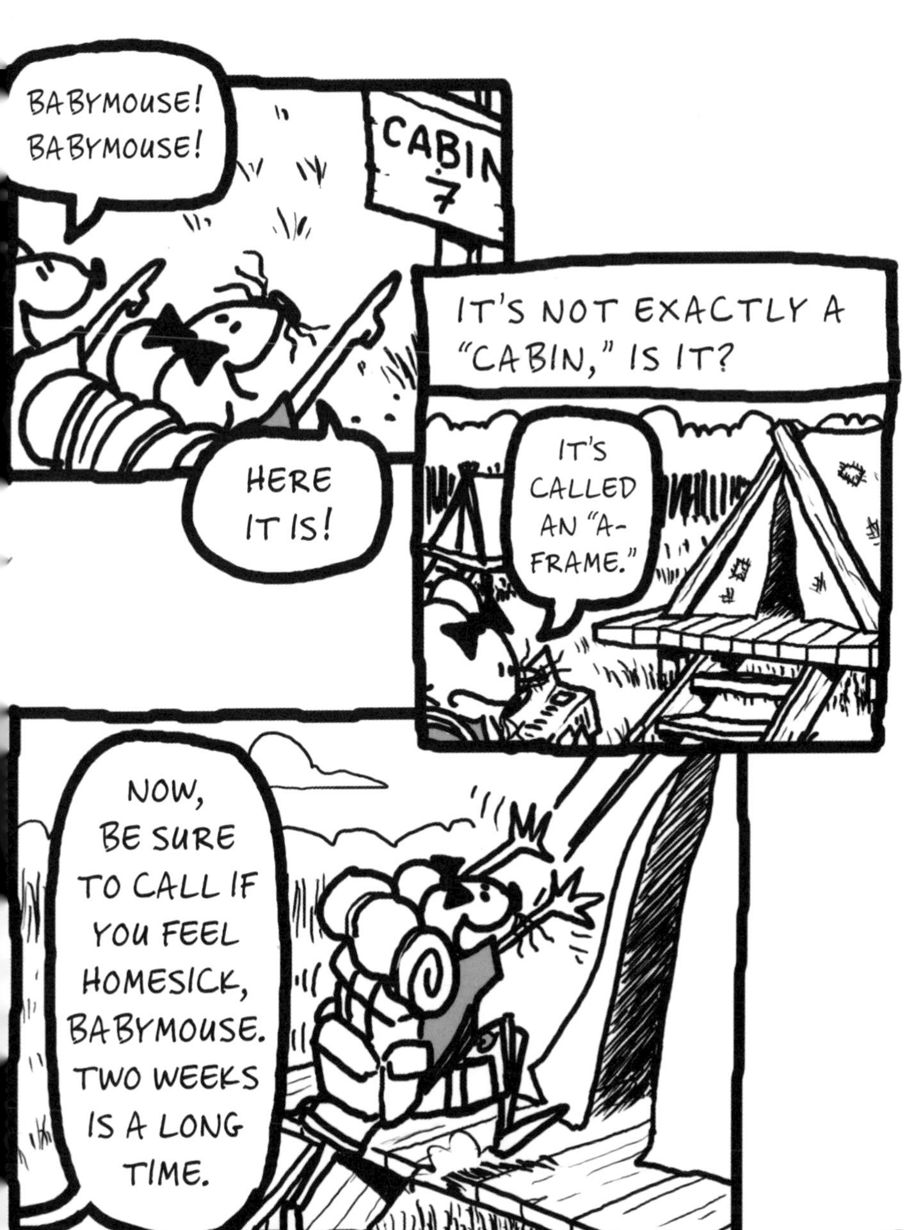
BABYMOUSE! BABYMOUSE!
CABIN 7
HERE IT IS!
IT'S NOT EXACTLY A "CABIN," IS IT?
IT'S CALLED AN "A-FRAME."
NOW, BE SURE TO CALL IF YOU FEEL HOMESICK, BABYMOUSE. TWO WEEKS IS A LONG TIME.

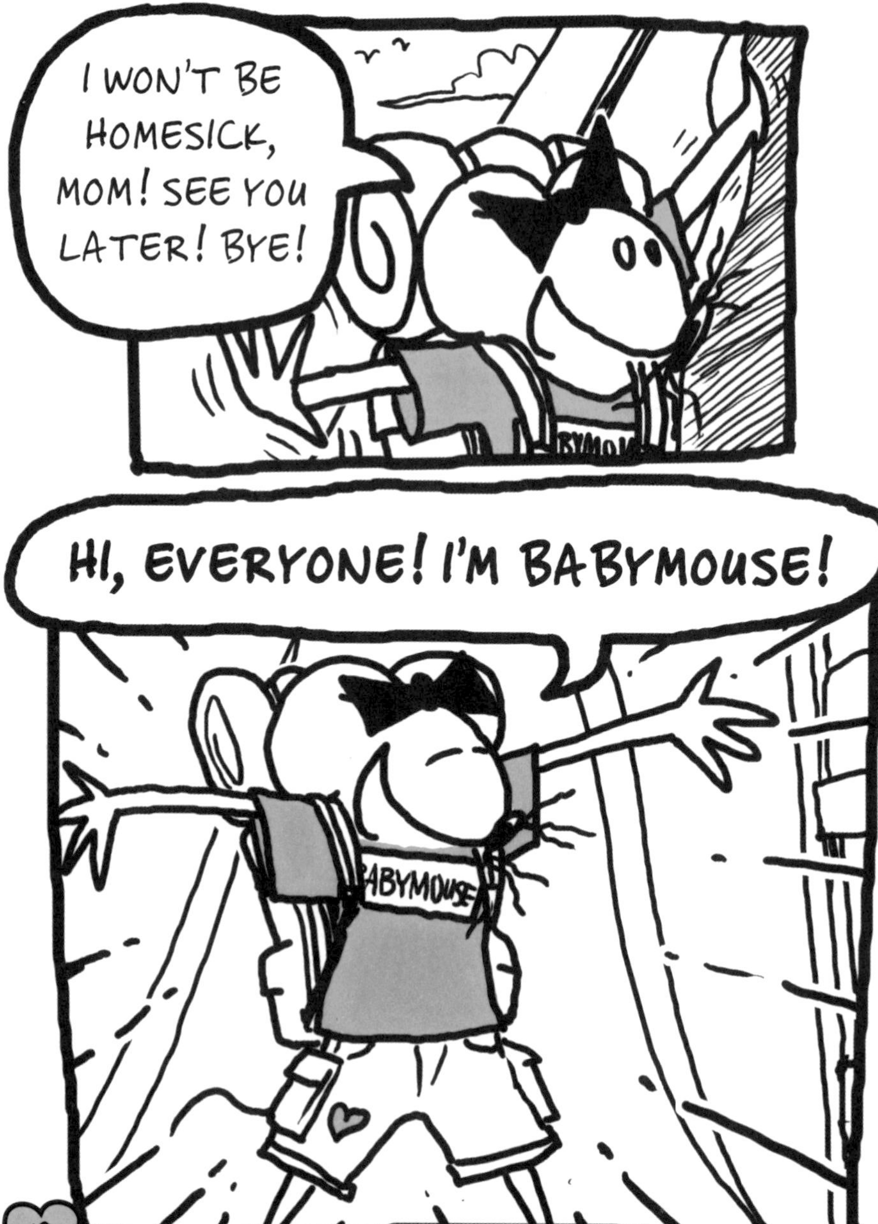
I WON'T BE HOMESICK, MOM! SEE YOU LATER! BYE!
BABYMOUSE
HI, EVERYONE! I'M BABYMOUSE!
BABYMOUSE

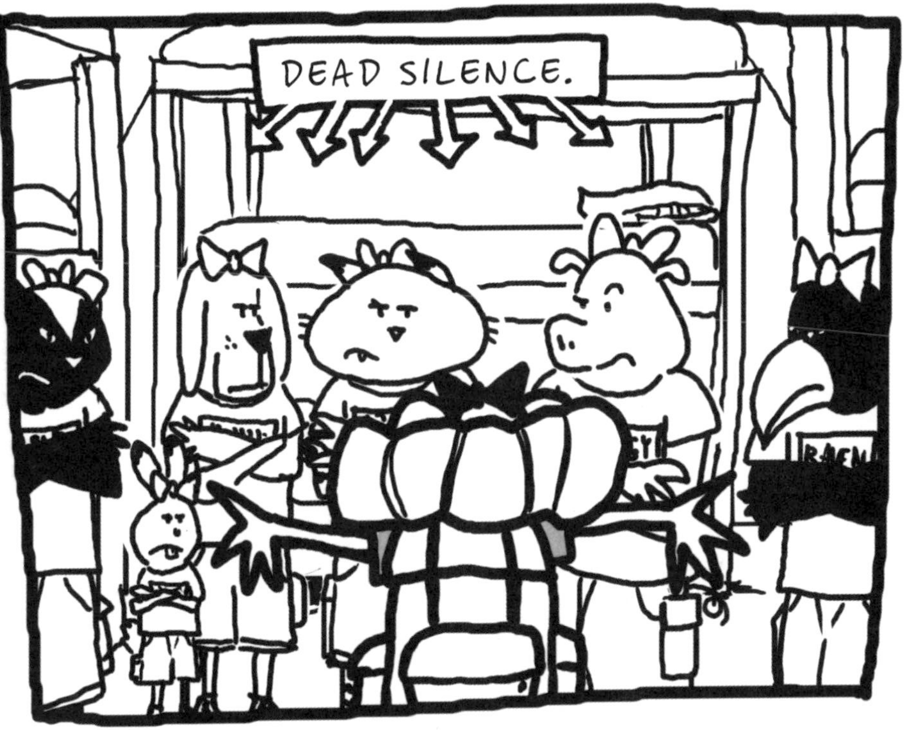
DEAD SILENCE.

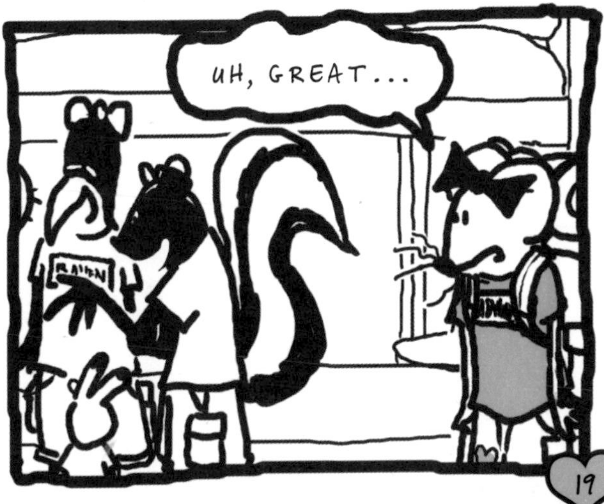
UH, GREAT...

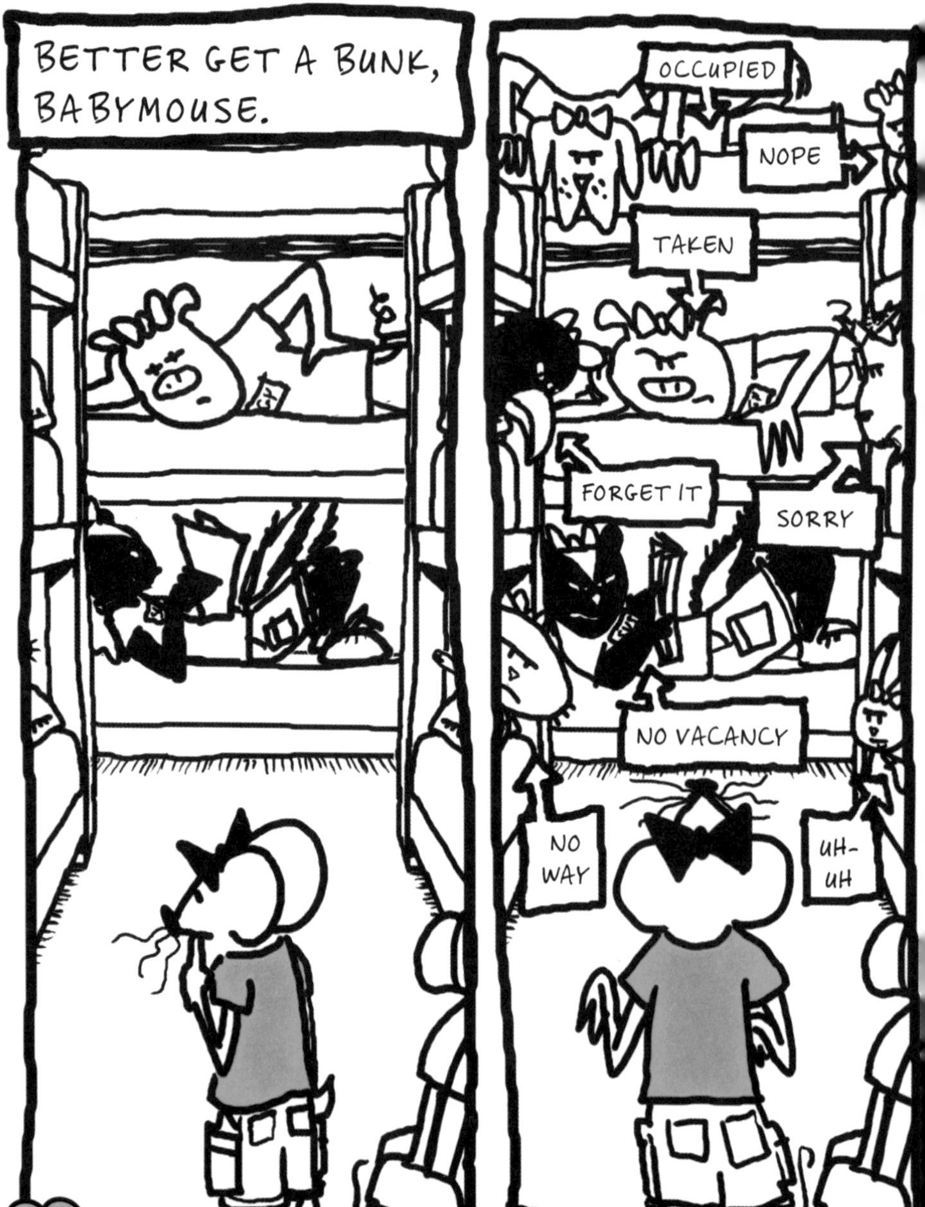
BETTER GET A BUNK, BABYMOUSE.
OCCUPIED
NOPE
TAKEN
FORGET IT
SORRY
NO VACANCY
NO WAY
UH-UH

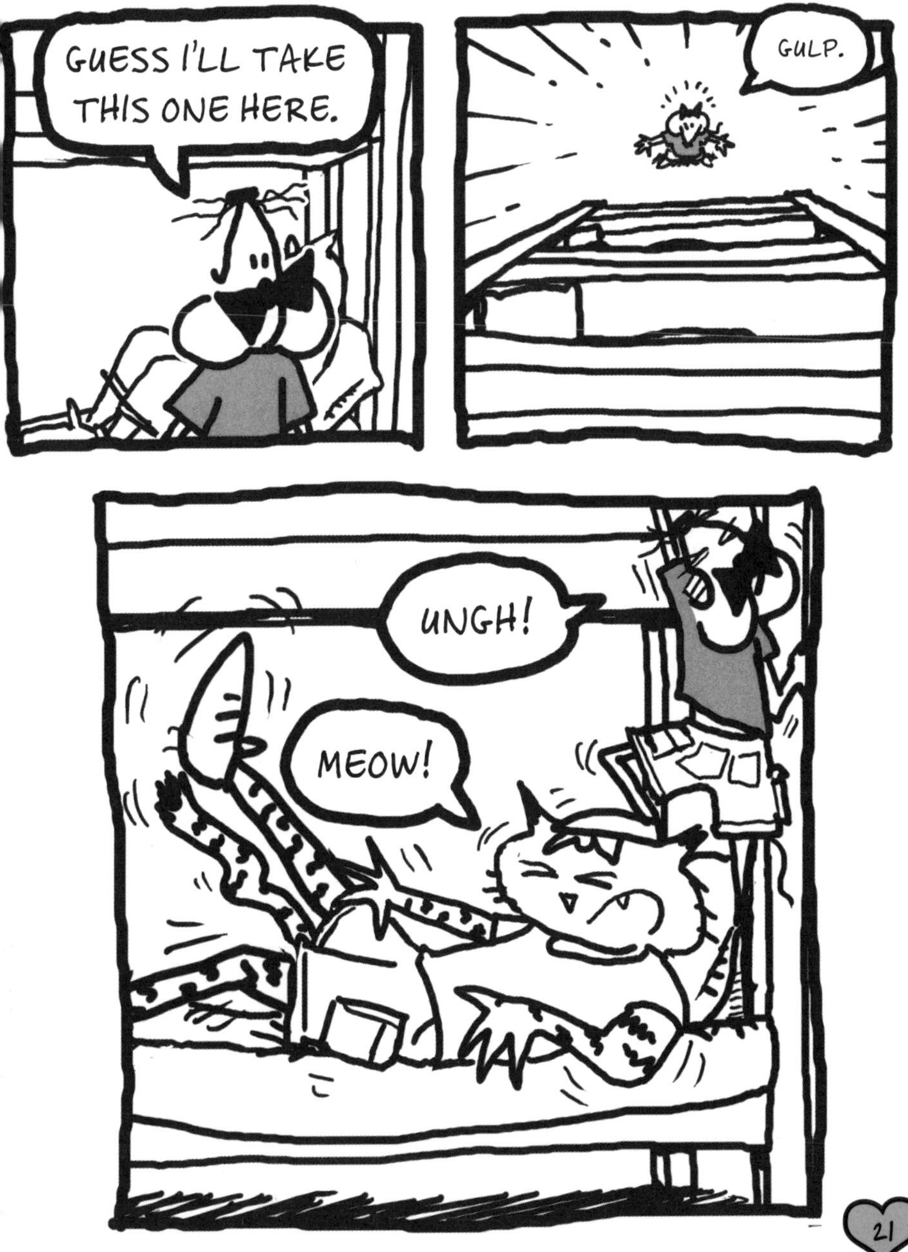
GUESS I'LL TAKE THIS ONE HERE.
GULP.
UNGH!
MEOW!

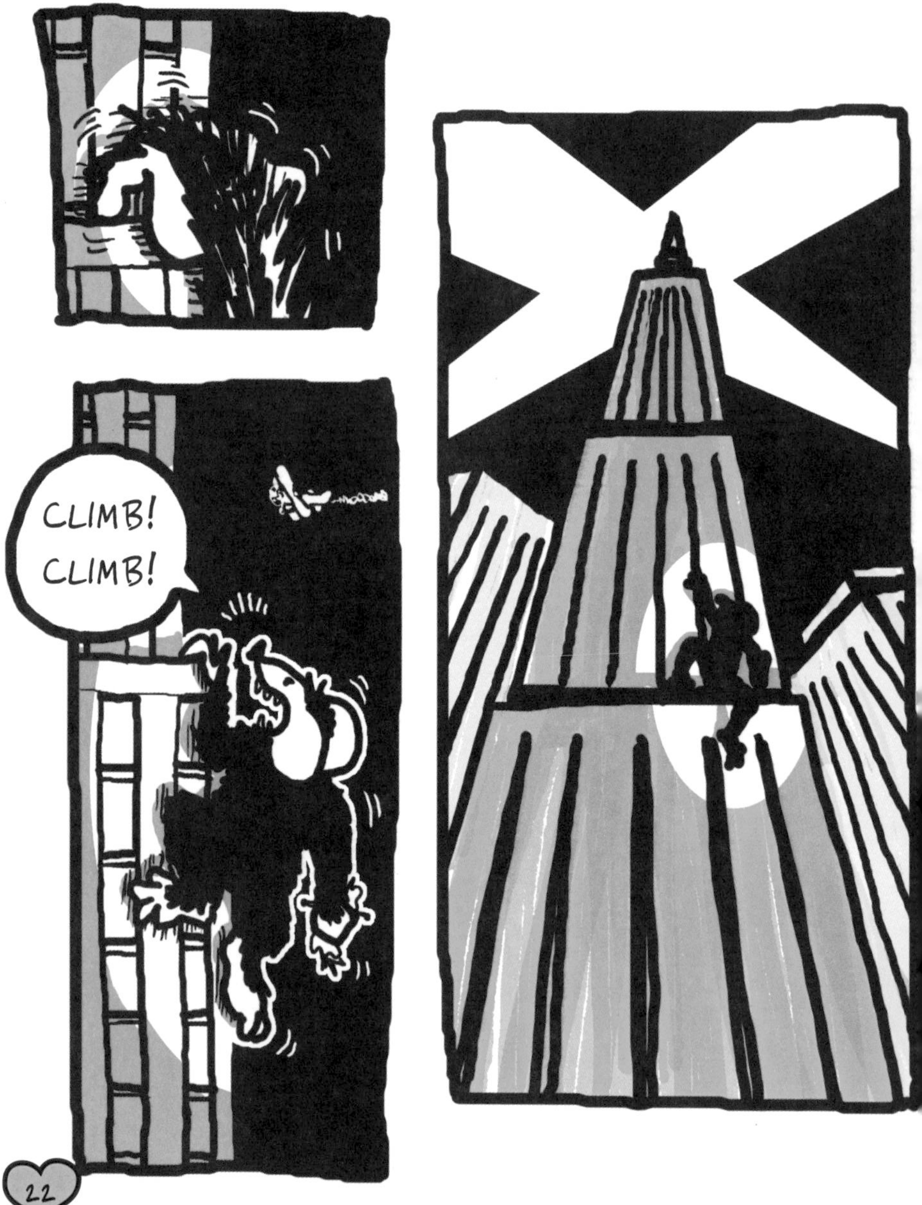
CLIMB!
CLIMB!

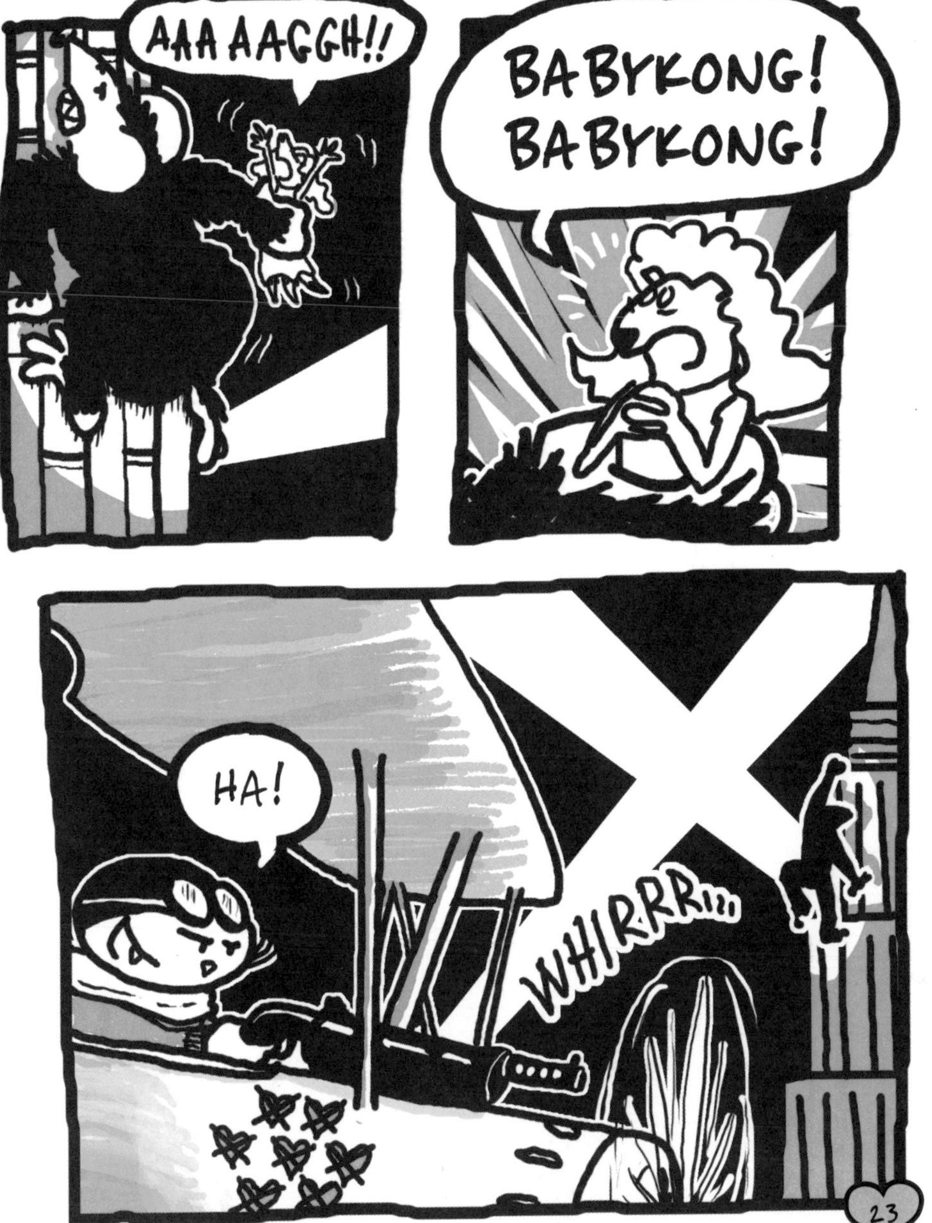
AAA AAGGH!!
BABYKONG! BABYKONG!
HA!
WHIRRR...

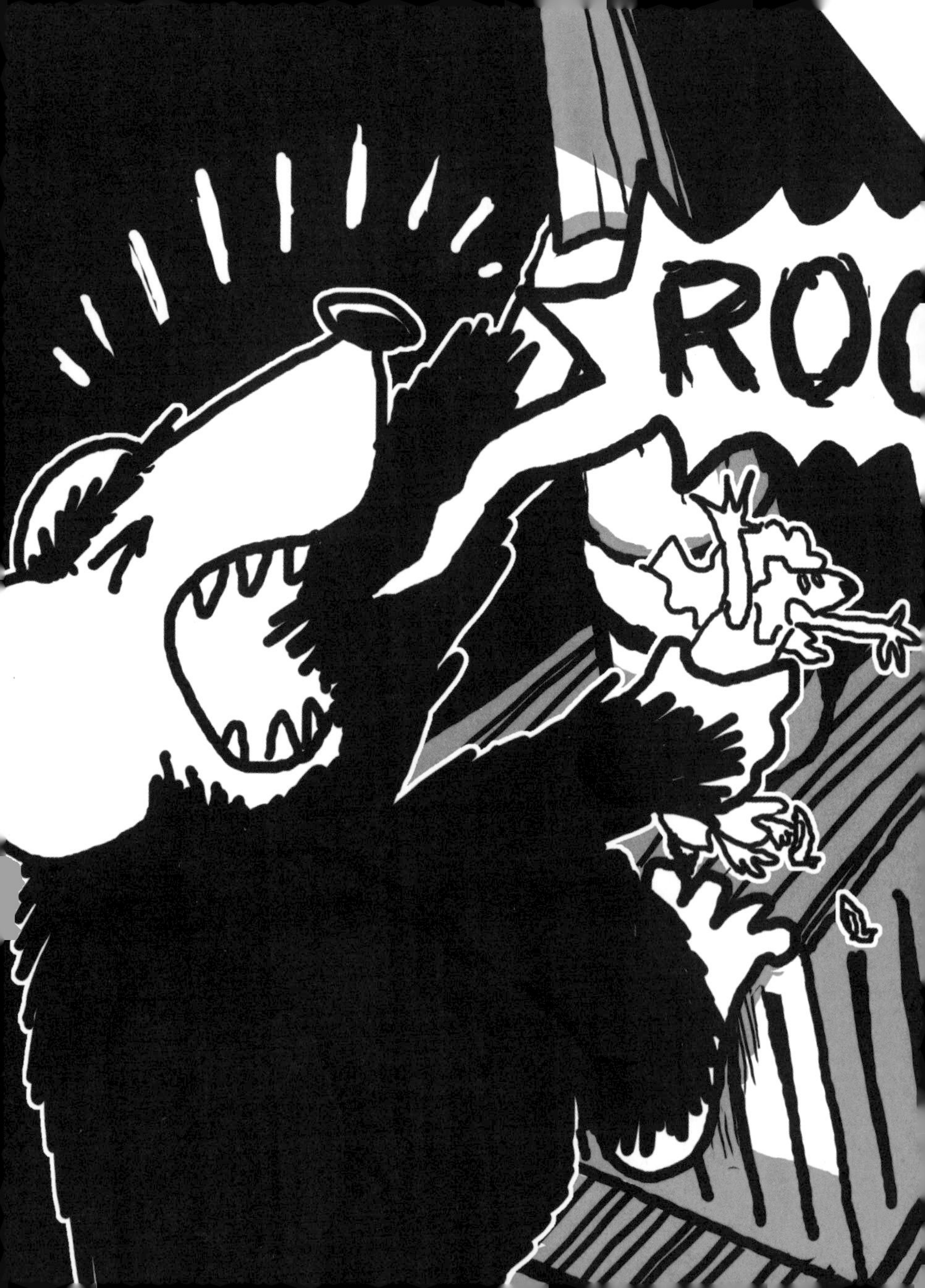
ROO

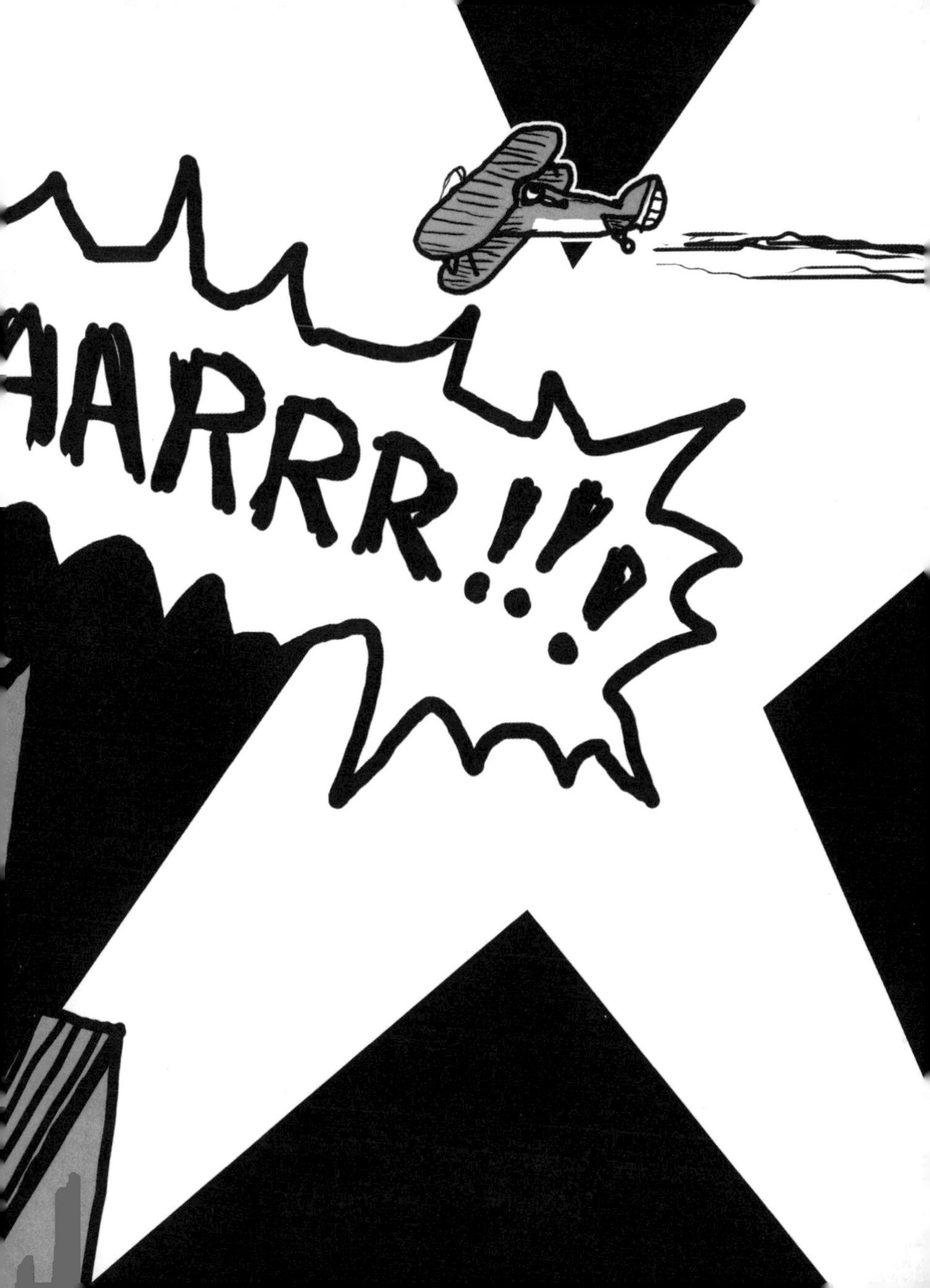
ARRRR!!!

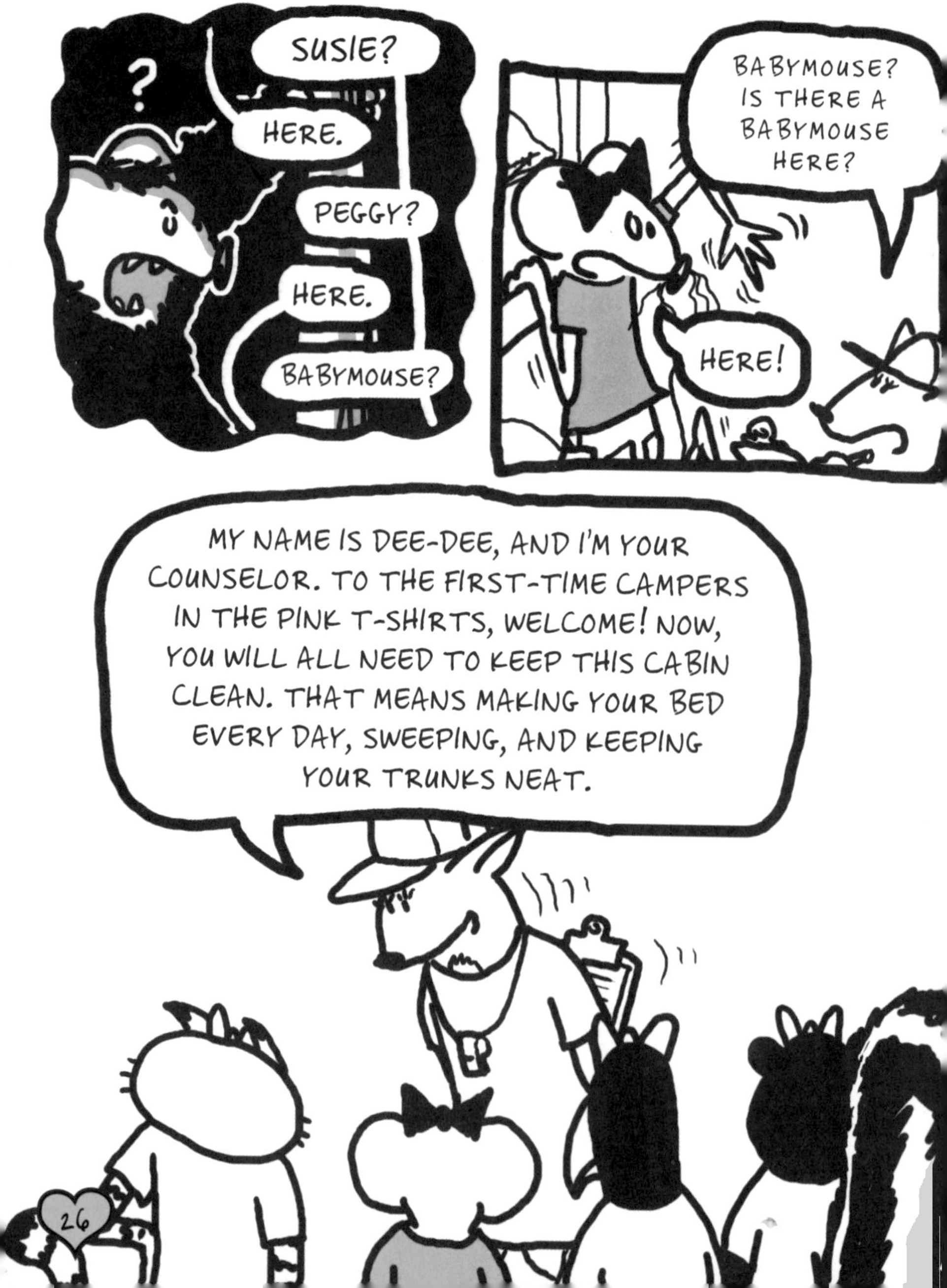
SUSIE?
HERE.
PEGGY?
HERE.
BABYMOUSE?
BABYMOUSE? IS THERE A BABYMOUSE HERE?
HERE!
MY NAME IS DEE-DEE, AND I'M YOUR COUNSELOR. TO THE FIRST-TIME CAMPERS IN THE PINK T-SHIRTS, WELCOME! NOW, YOU WILL ALL NEED TO KEEP THIS CABIN CLEAN. THAT MEANS MAKING YOUR BED EVERY DAY, SWEEPING, AND KEEPING YOUR TRUNKS NEAT.

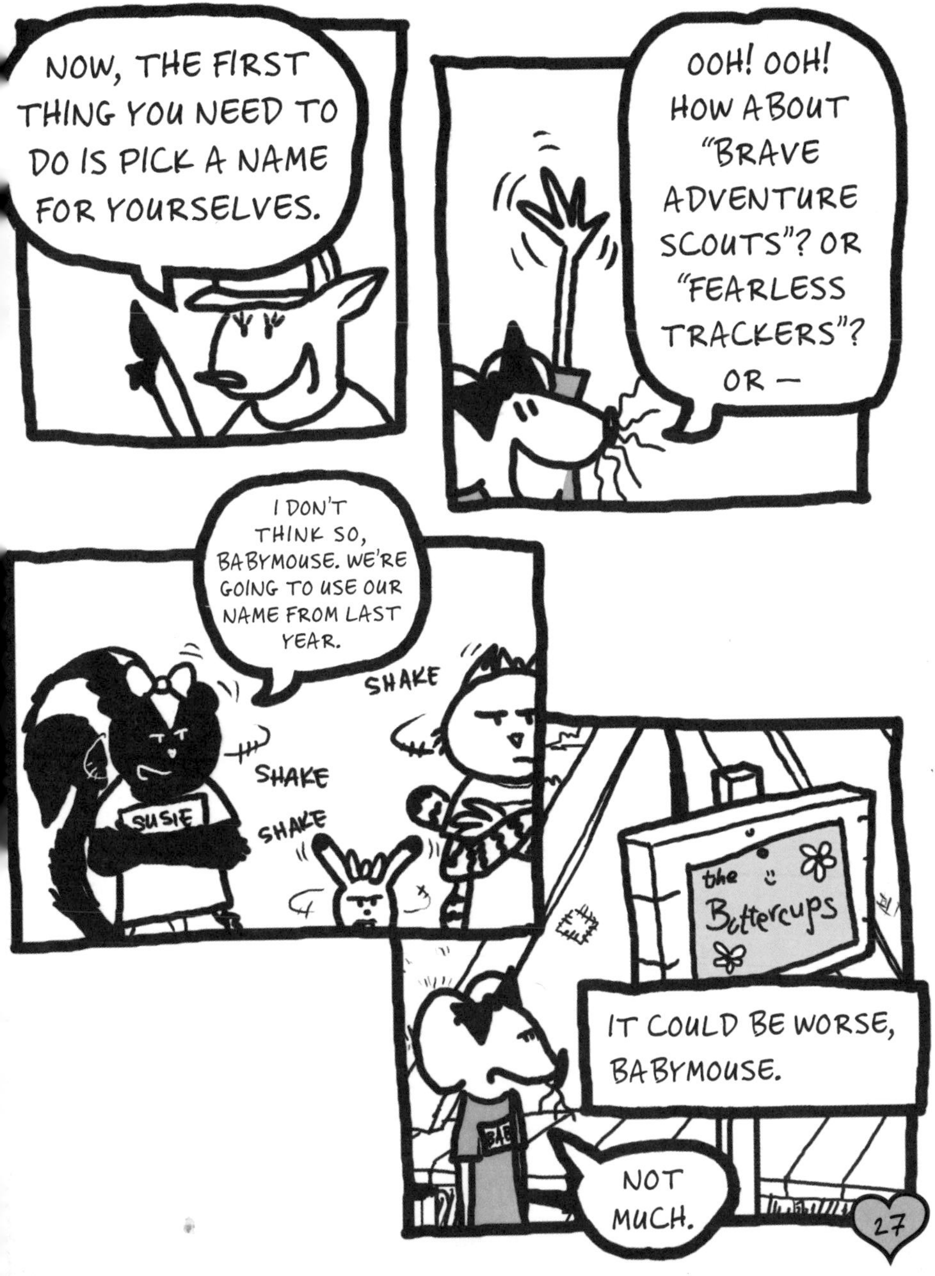

NOW, THE FIRST THING YOU NEED TO DO IS PICK A NAME FOR YOURSELVES.
OOH! OOH! HOW ABOUT "BRAVE ADVENTURE SCOUTS"? OR "FEARLESS TRACKERS"? OR —
I DON'T THINK SO, BABYMOUSE. WE'RE GOING TO USE OUR NAME FROM LAST YEAR.
SHAKE
SHAKE
SHAKE
SUSIE
the Buttercups
IT COULD BE WORSE, BABYMOUSE.
NOT MUCH.

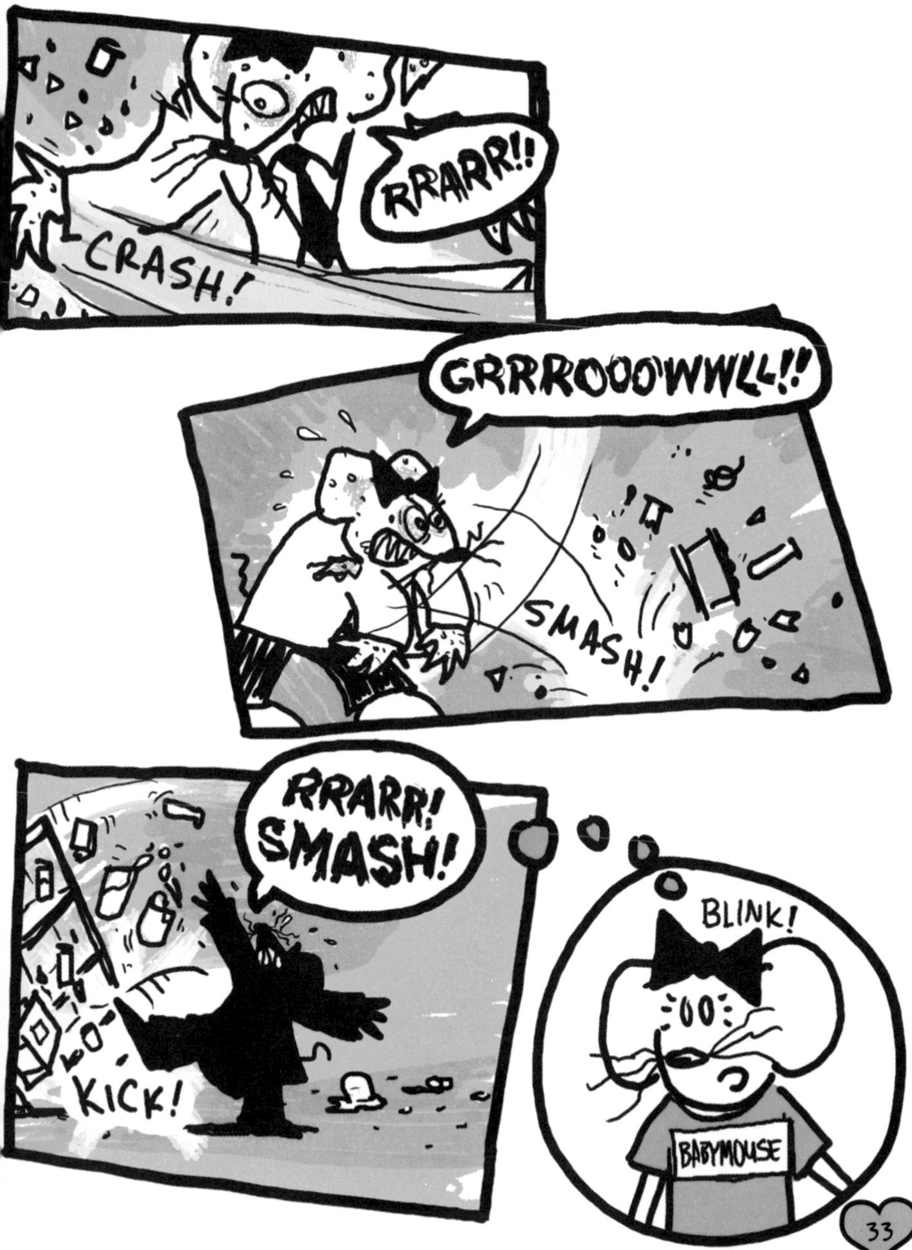
RRARR!!
CRASH!
GRRROOOWWLL!!
SMASH!
RRARR!
SMASH!
KICK!
BLINK!
BABYMOUSE

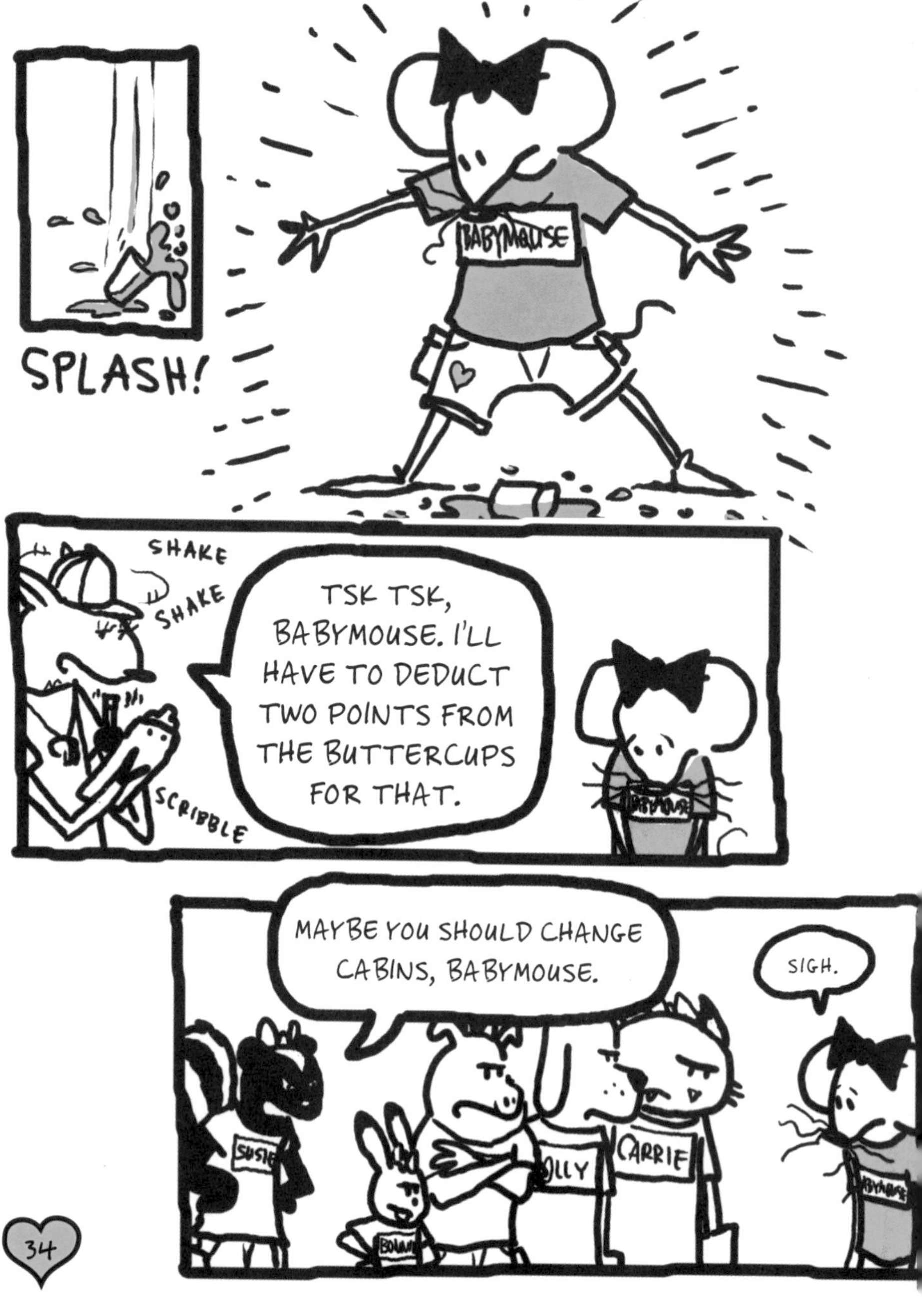

SPLASH!
BABYMOUSE
SHAKE
SHAKE
TSK TSK, BABYMOUSE. I'LL HAVE TO DEDUCT TWO POINTS FROM THE BUTTERCUPS FOR THAT.
SCRIBBLE
BABYMOUSE
MAYBE YOU SHOULD CHANGE CABINS, BABYMOUSE.
SIGH.
SUSIE
CARRIE

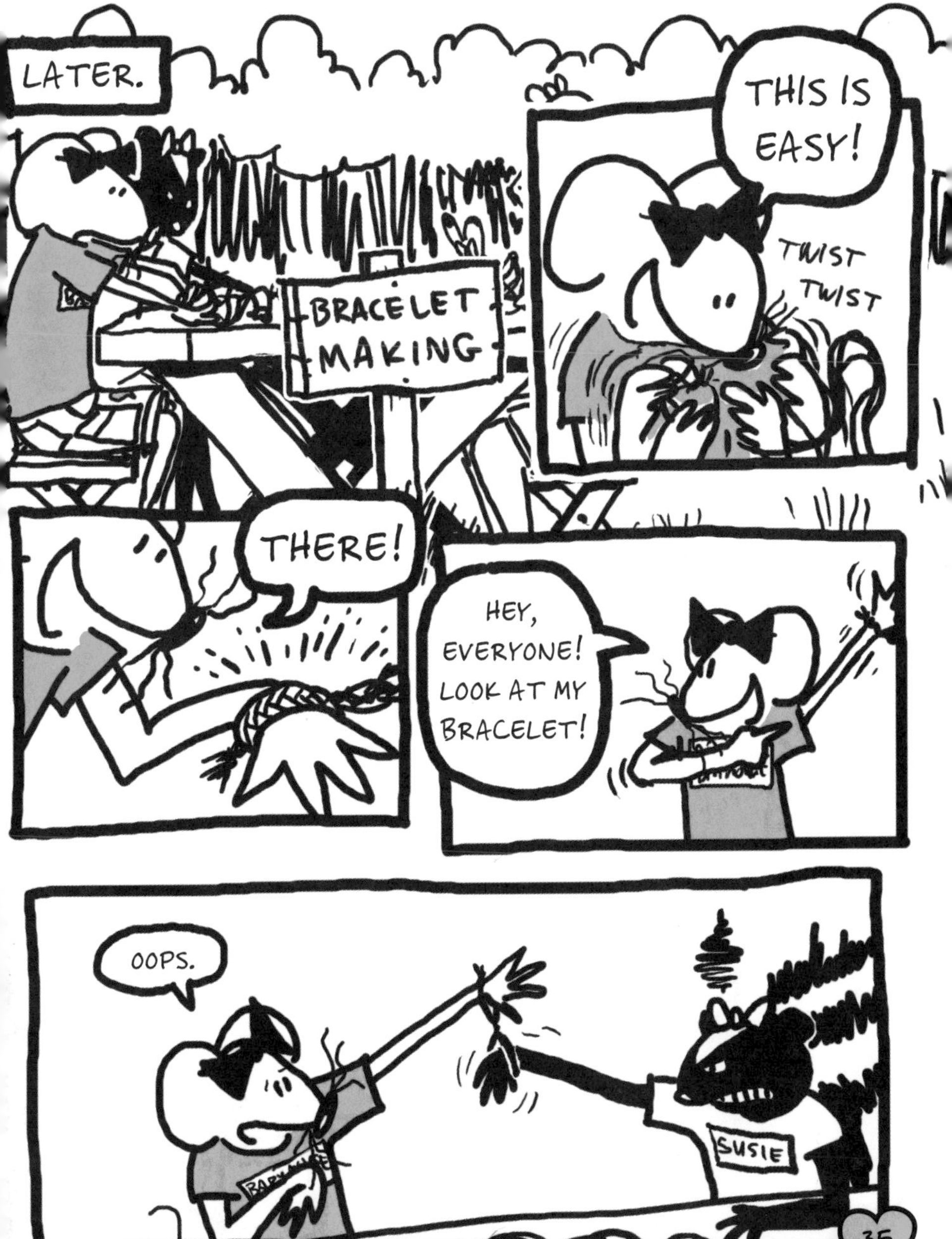
LATER.
BRACELET MAKING
THIS IS EASY!
TWIST TWIST
THERE!
HEY, EVERYONE! LOOK AT MY BRACELET!
OOPS.
SUSIE

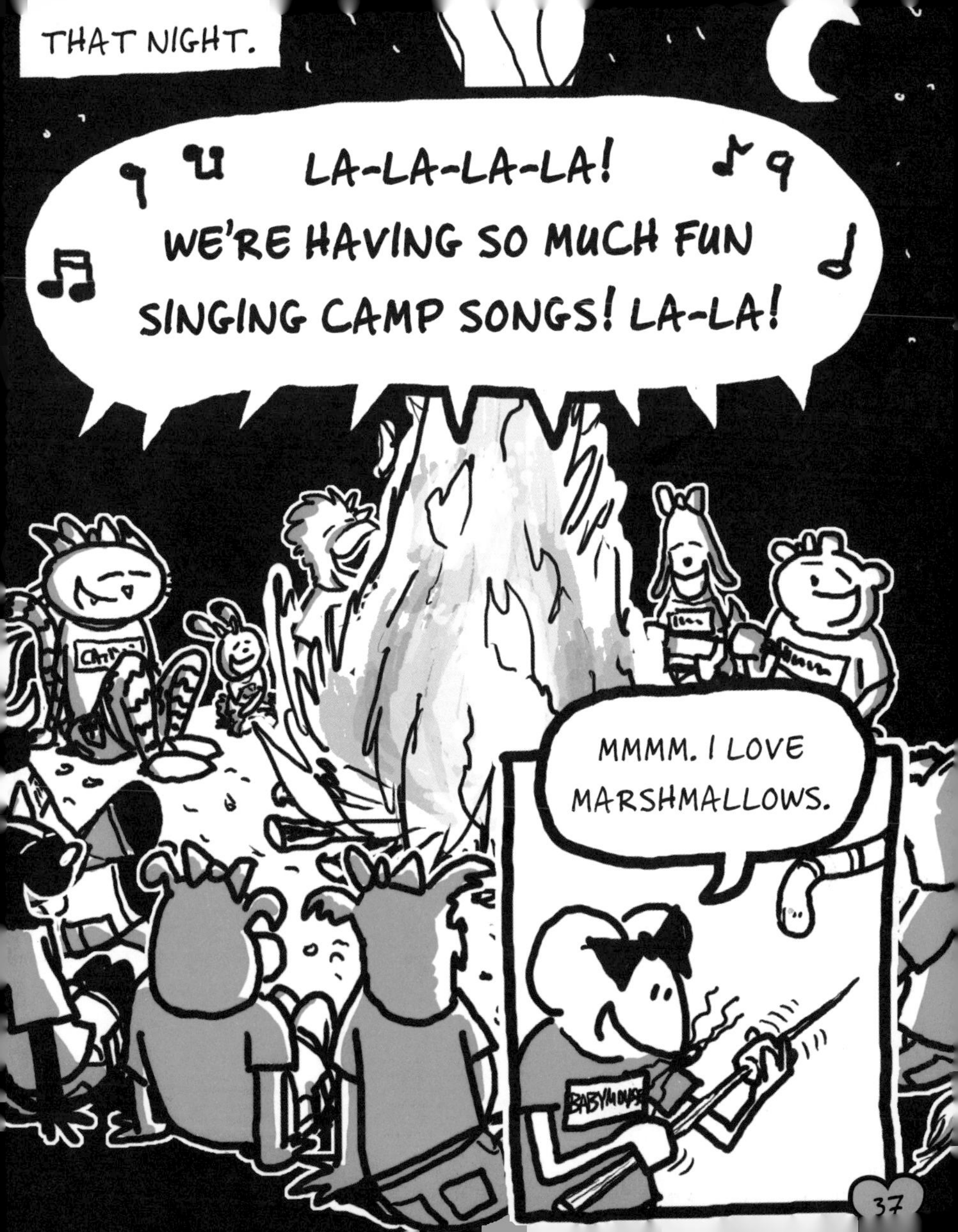
THAT NIGHT.
LA-LA-LA-LA! WE'RE HAVING SO MUCH FUN SINGING CAMP SONGS! LA-LA!
MMMM. I LOVE MARSHMALLOWS.
BABYMOUSE

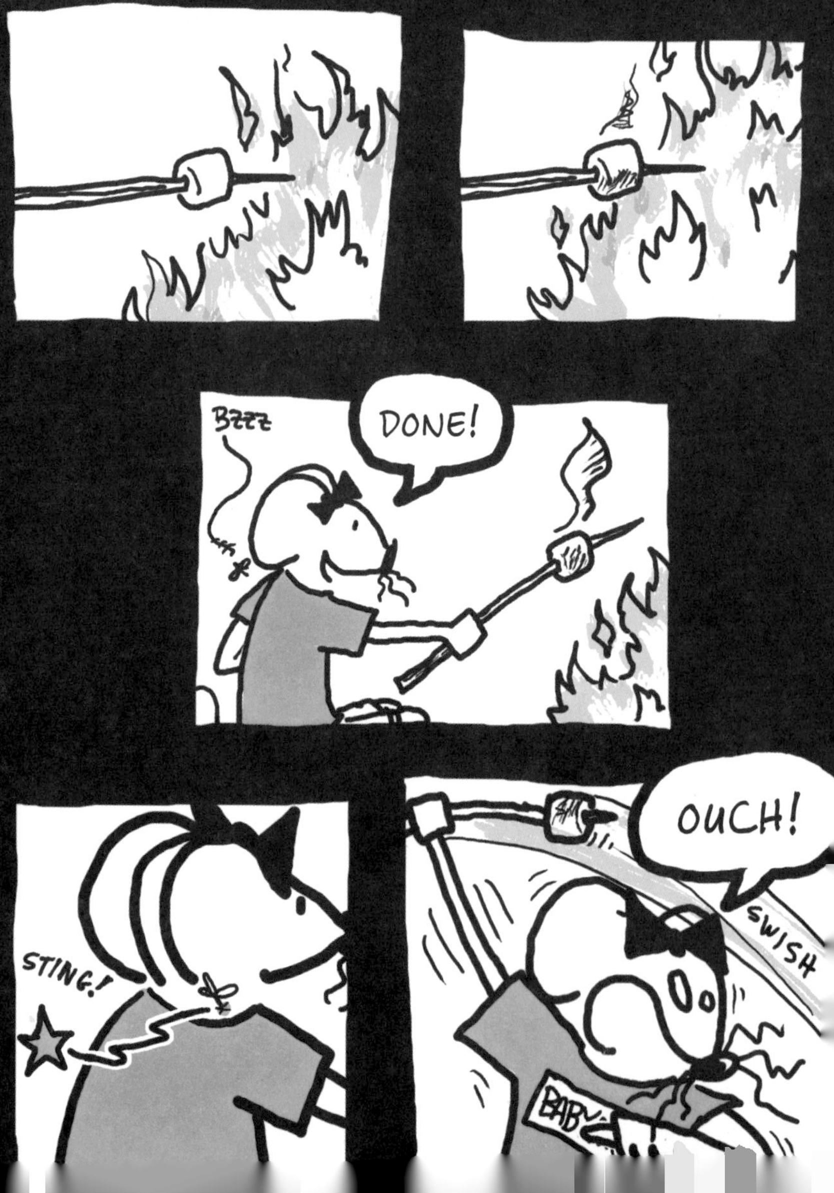
BZZZ
DONE!
STING!
OUCH!
SWISH
BABY

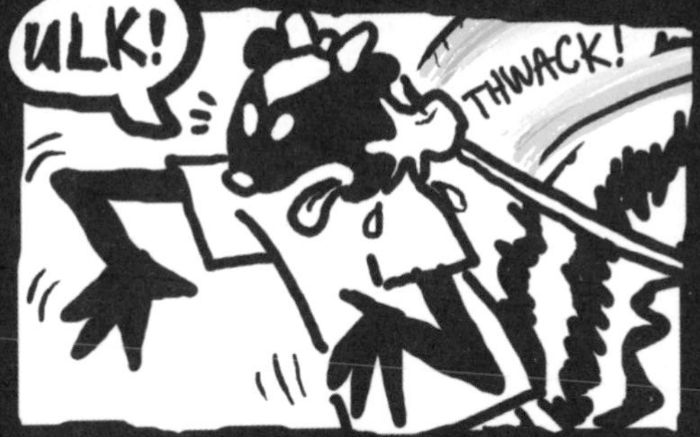
ULK!
THWACK!

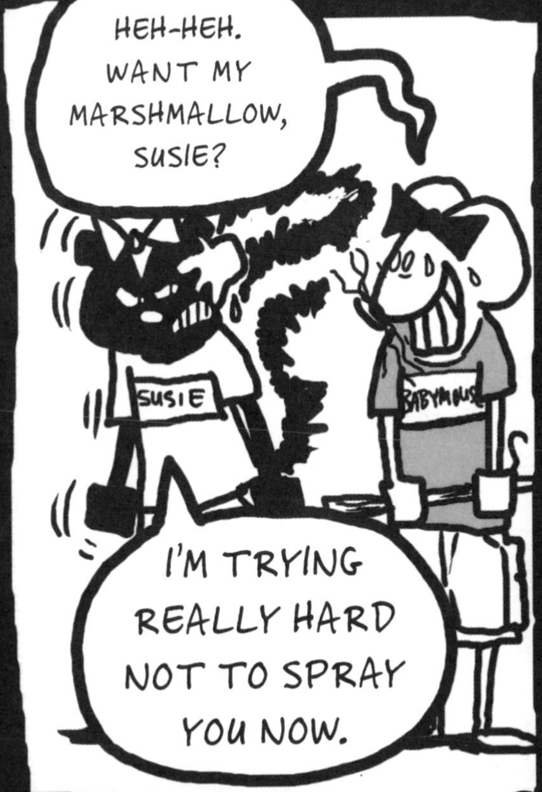
HEH-HEH. WANT MY MARSHMALLOW, SUSIE?
SUSIE
I'M TRYING REALLY HARD NOT TO SPRAY YOU NOW.

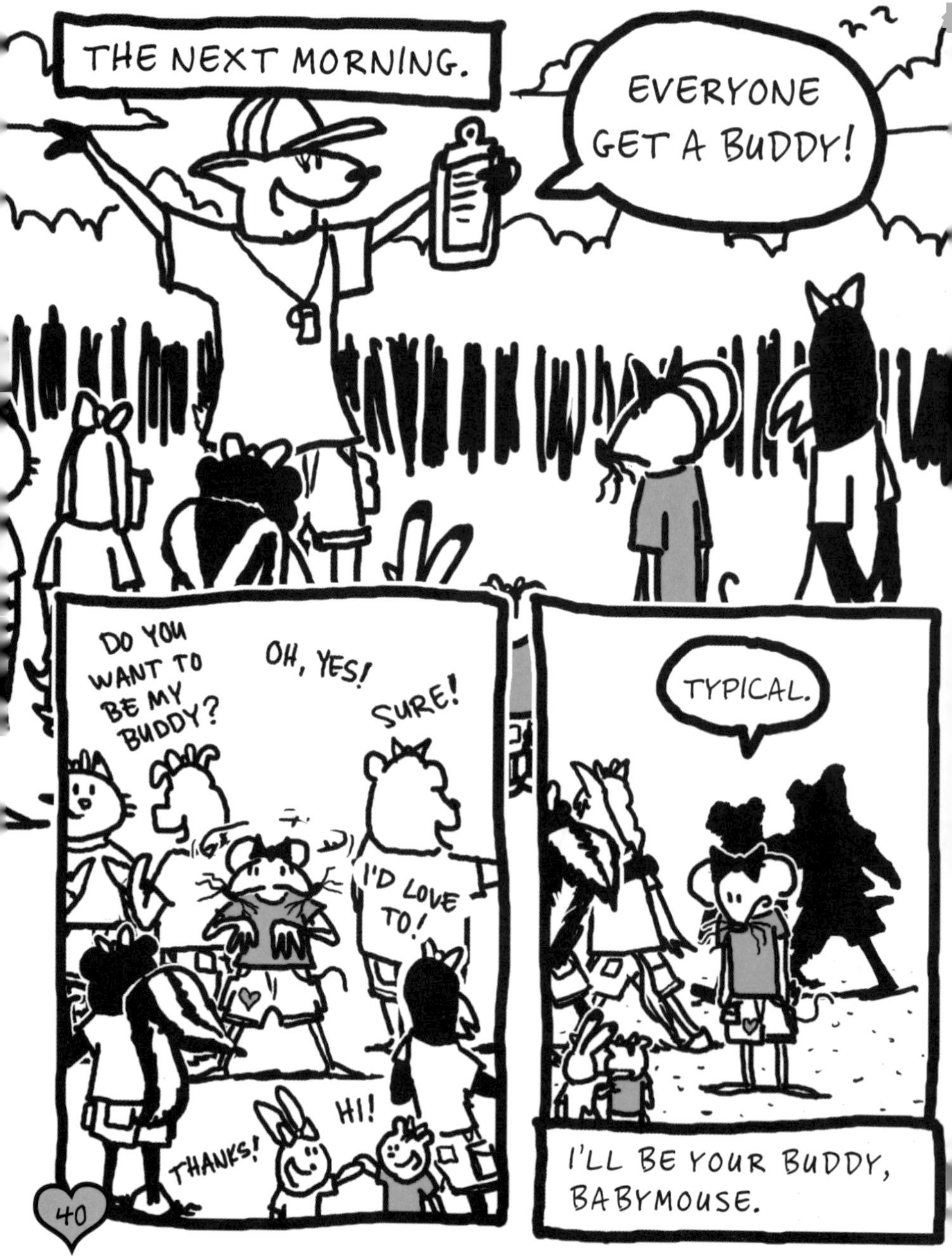

THE NEXT MORNING.
EVERYONE GET A BUDDY!
DO YOU WANT TO BE MY BUDDY?
OH, YES!
SURE!
I'D LOVE TO!
THANKS!
HI!
TYPICAL.
I'LL BE YOUR BUDDY, BABYMOUSE.

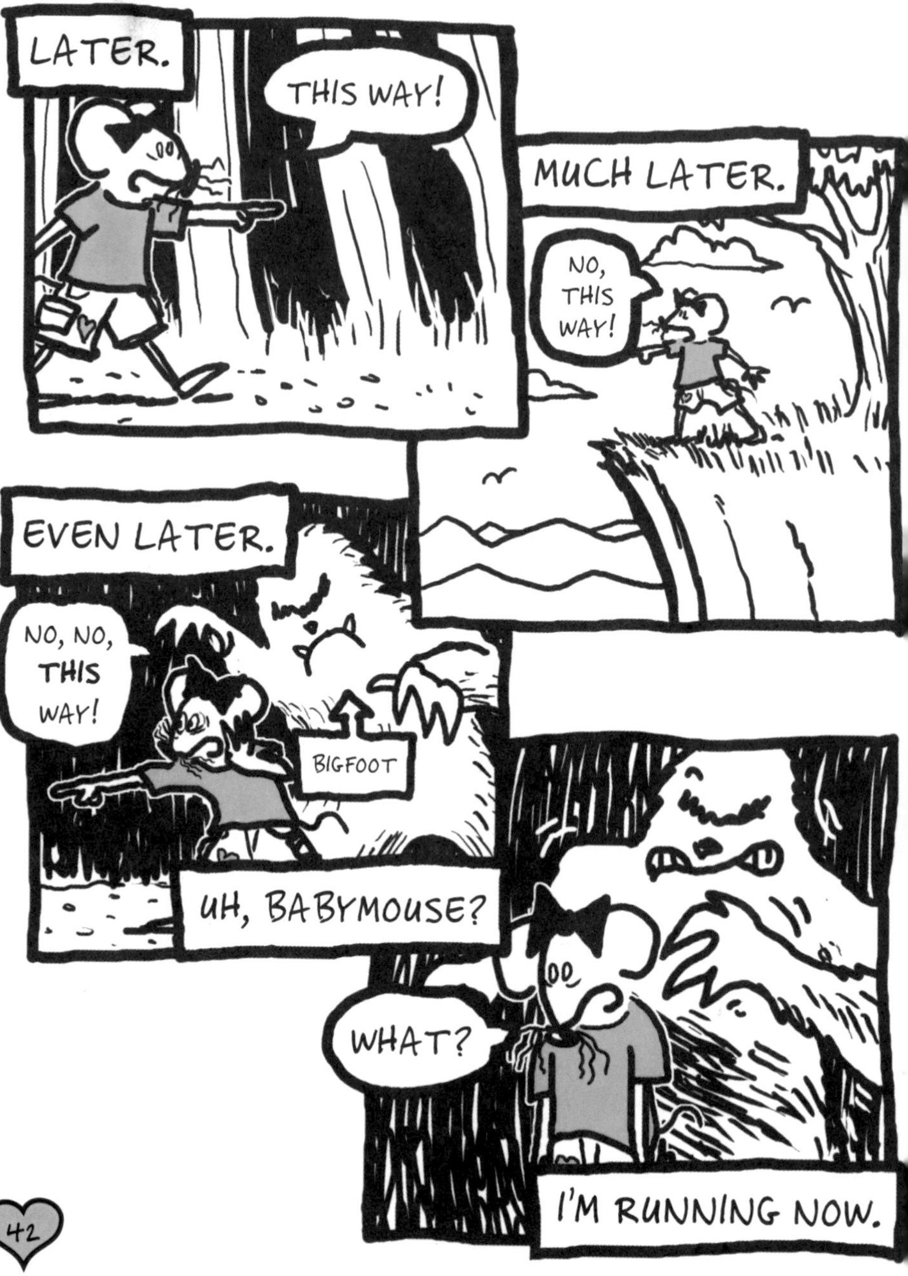
LATER.
THIS WAY!
MUCH LATER.
NO, THIS WAY!
EVEN LATER.
NO, NO, THIS WAY!
BIGFOOT
UH, BABYMOUSE?
WHAT?
I'M RUNNING NOW.

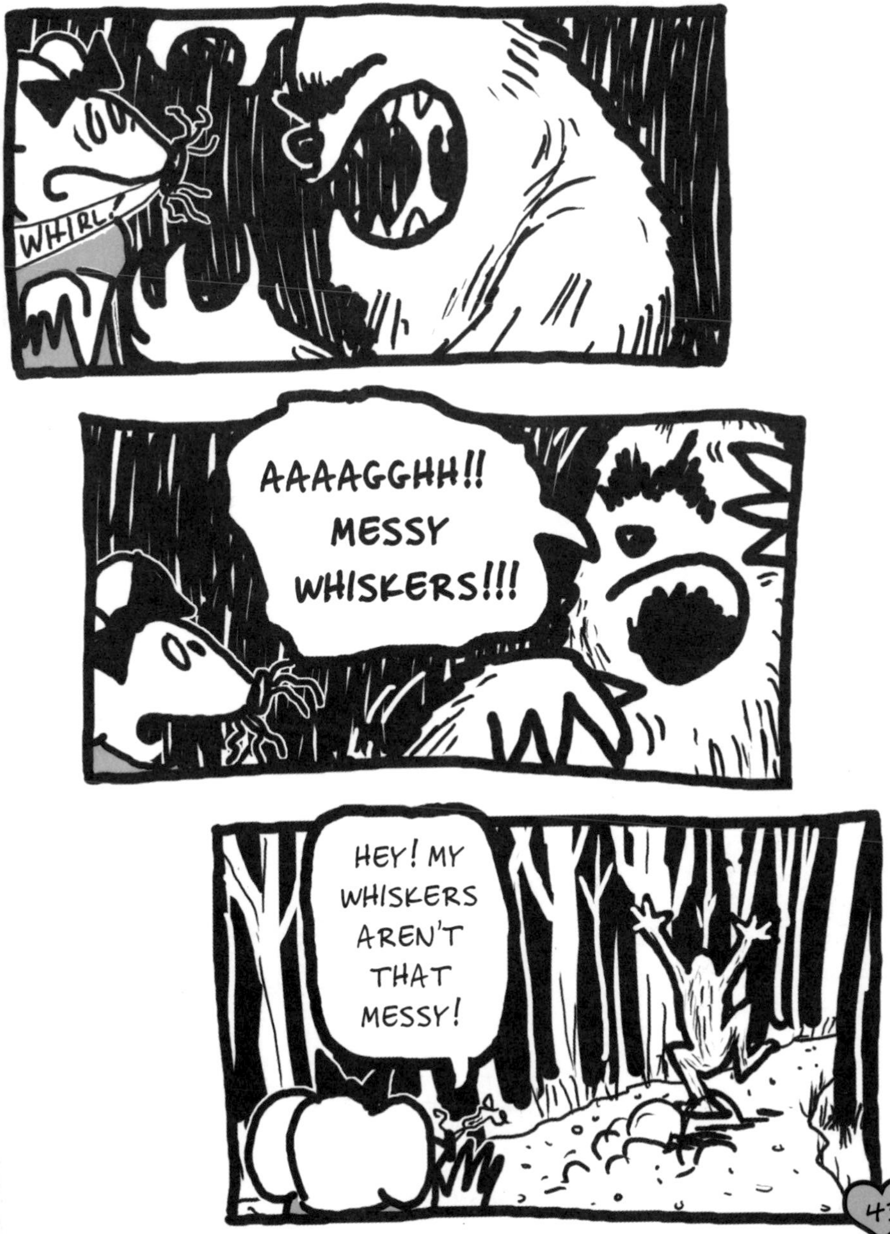
WHIRL!
AAAAGGHH!! MESSY WHISKERS!!!
HEY! MY WHISKERS AREN'T THAT MESSY!

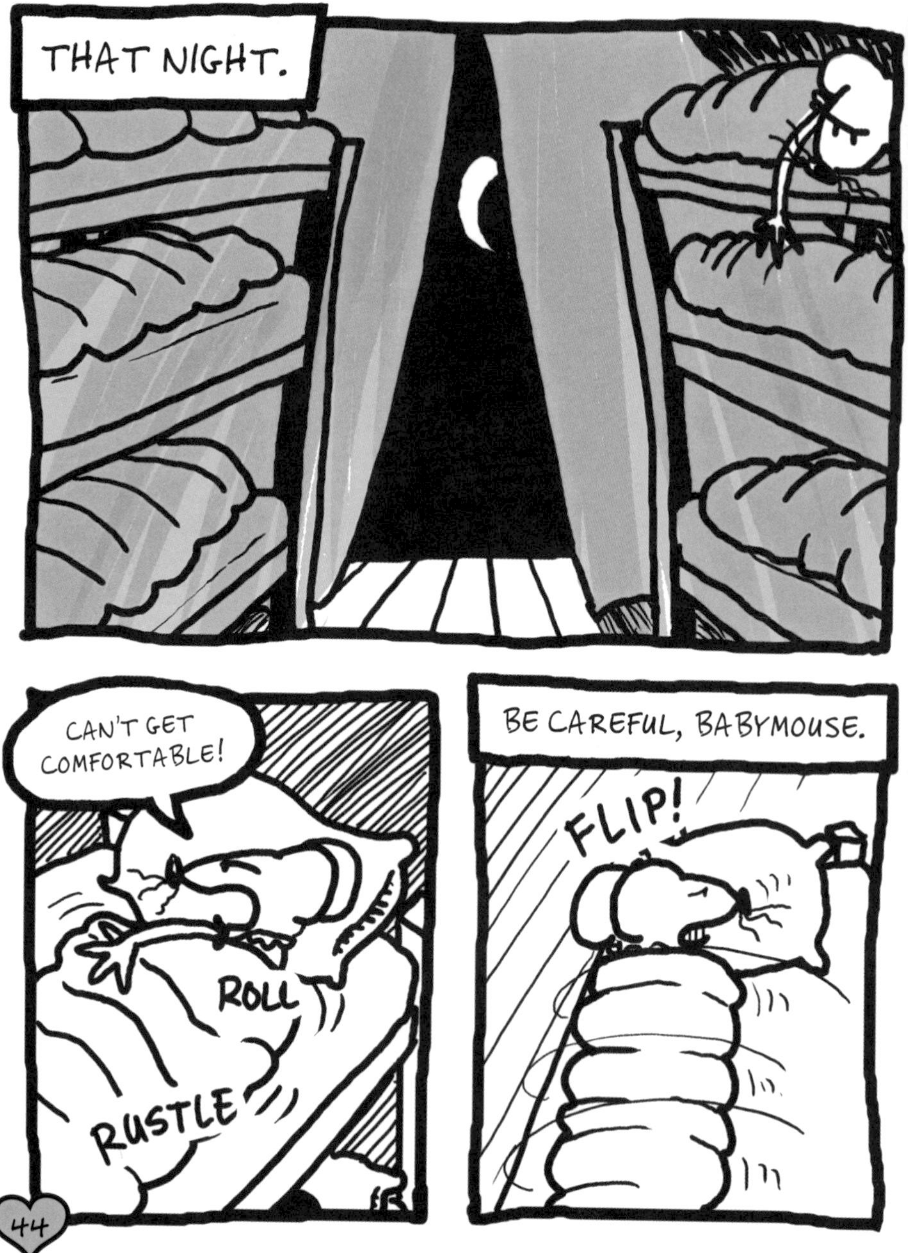
THAT NIGHT.
CAN'T GET COMFORTABLE!
ROLL
RUSTLE
BE CAREFUL, BABYMOUSE.
FLIP!

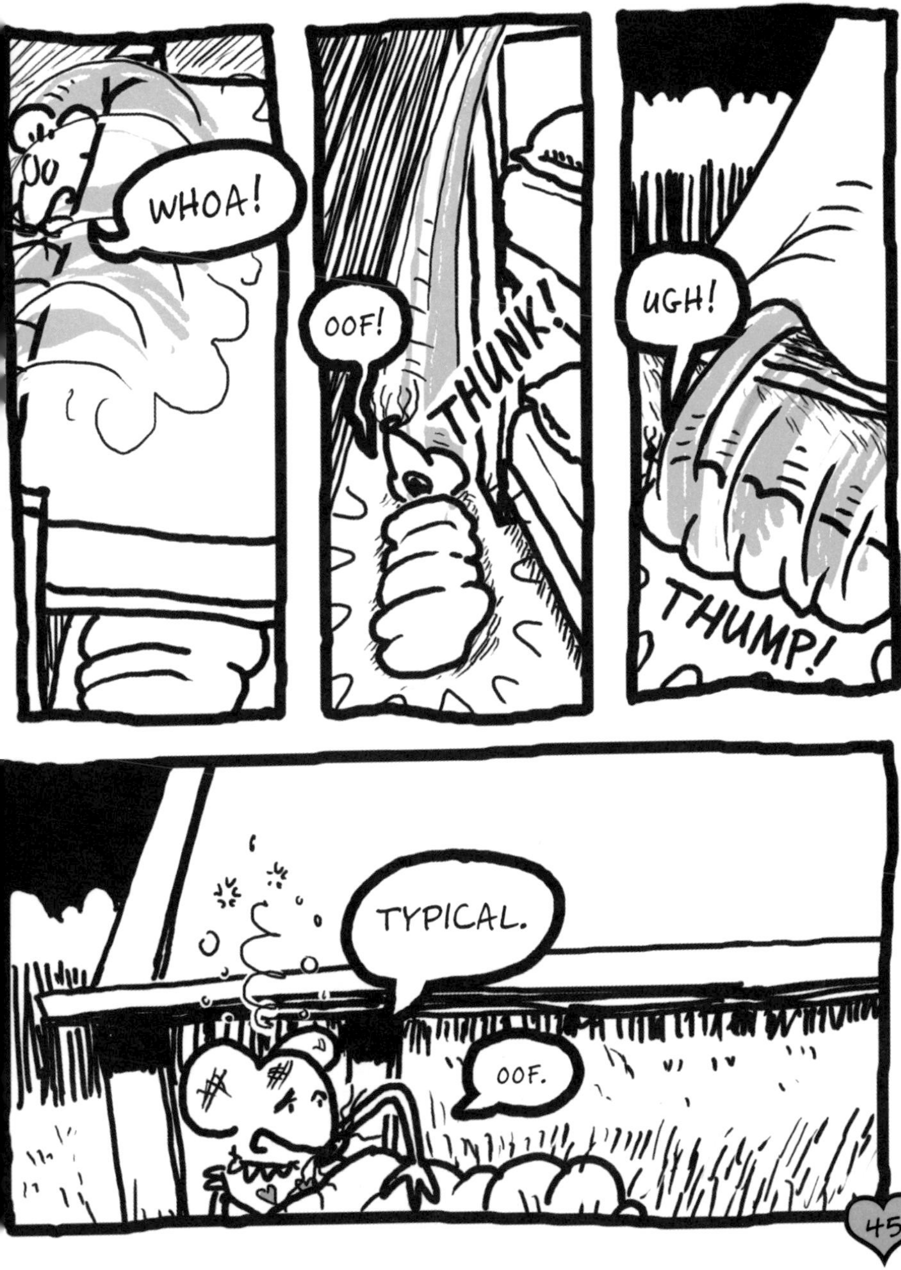
WHOA!
OOF!
THUNK!
UGH!
THUMP!
TYPICAL.
OOF.

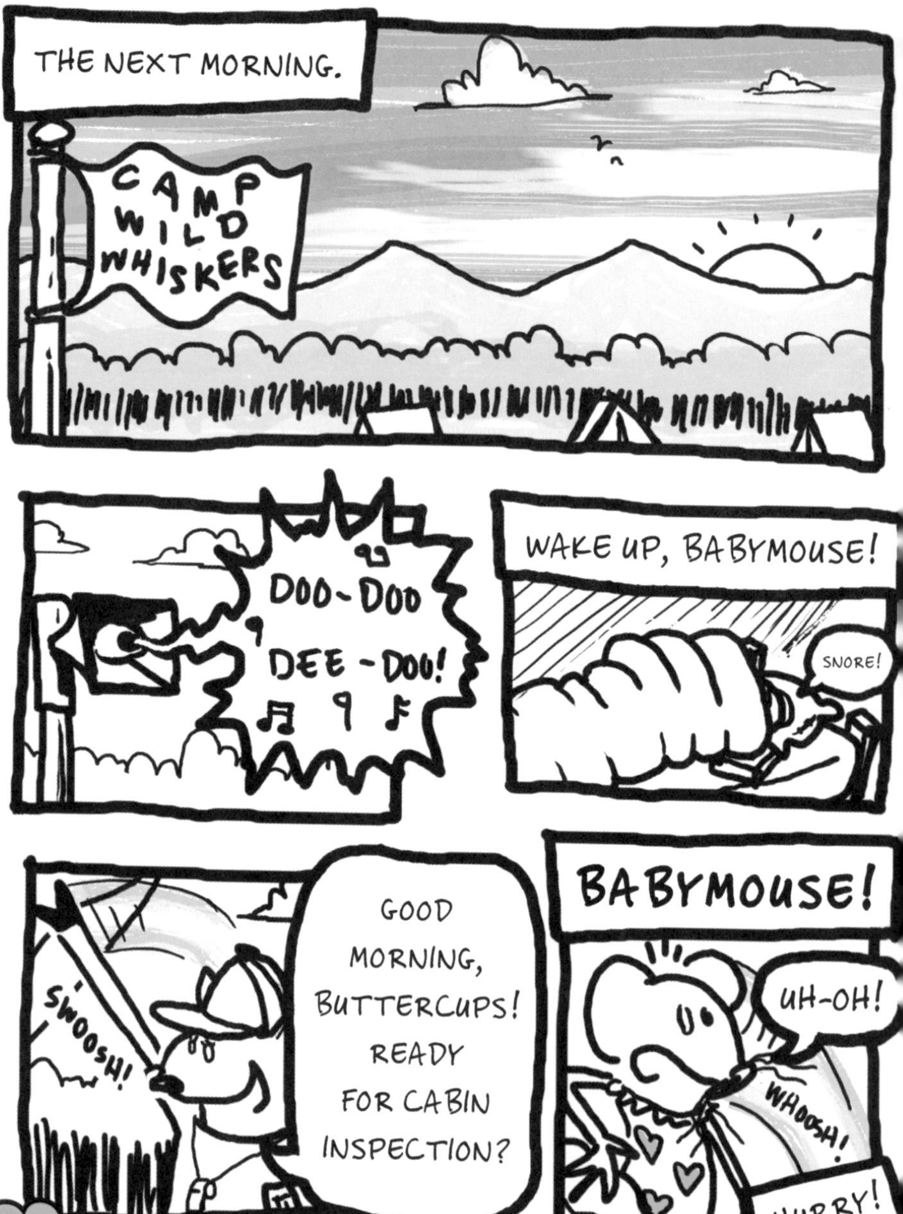
THE NEXT MORNING.
CAMP WILD WHISKERS
DOO-DOO DEE-DOO!
WAKE UP, BABYMOUSE!
SNORE!
SWOOSH!
GOOD MORNING, BUTTERCUPS! READY FOR CABIN INSPECTION?
BABYMOUSE!
UH-OH!
WHOOSH!
HURRY!

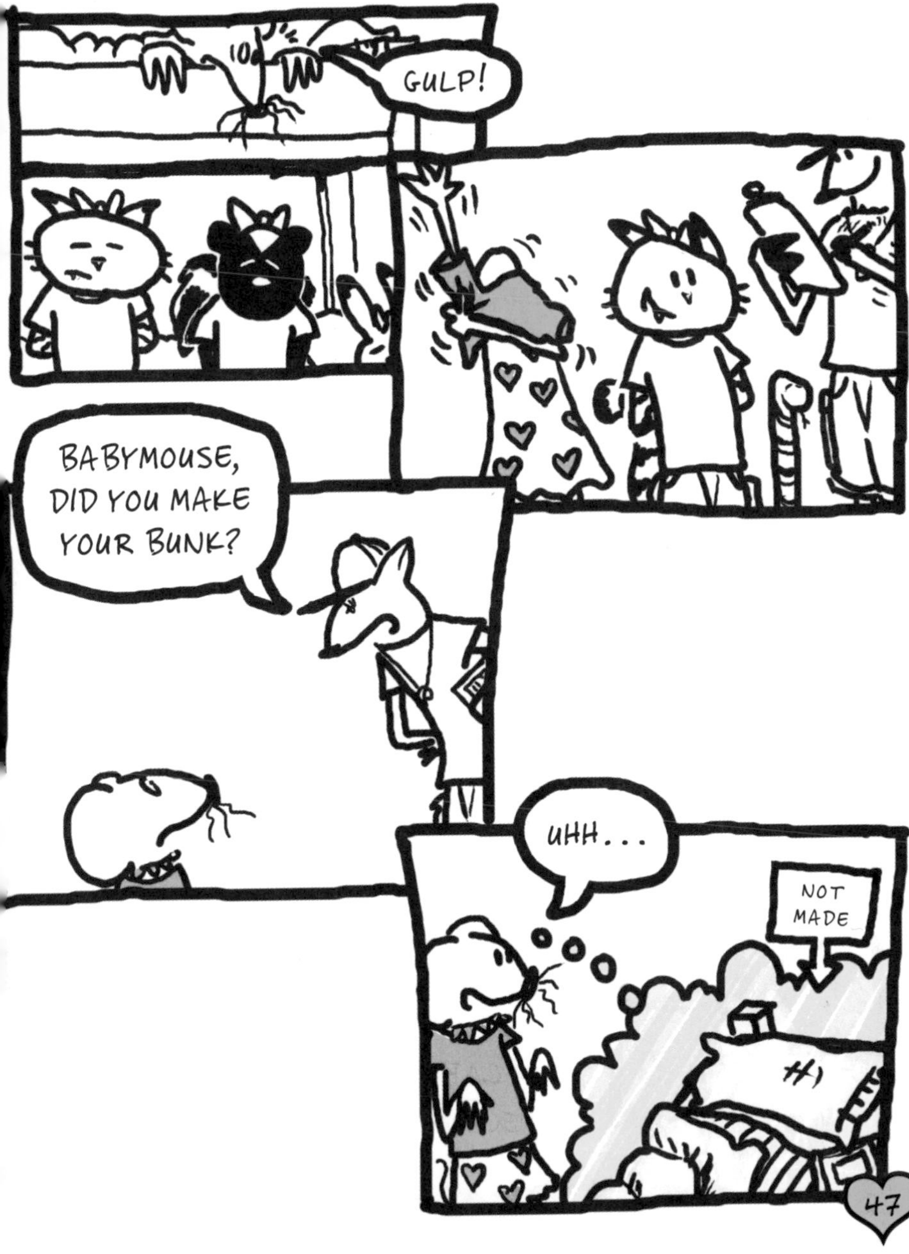
GULP!
BABYMOUSE, DID YOU MAKE YOUR BUNK?
UHH . . .
NOT MADE

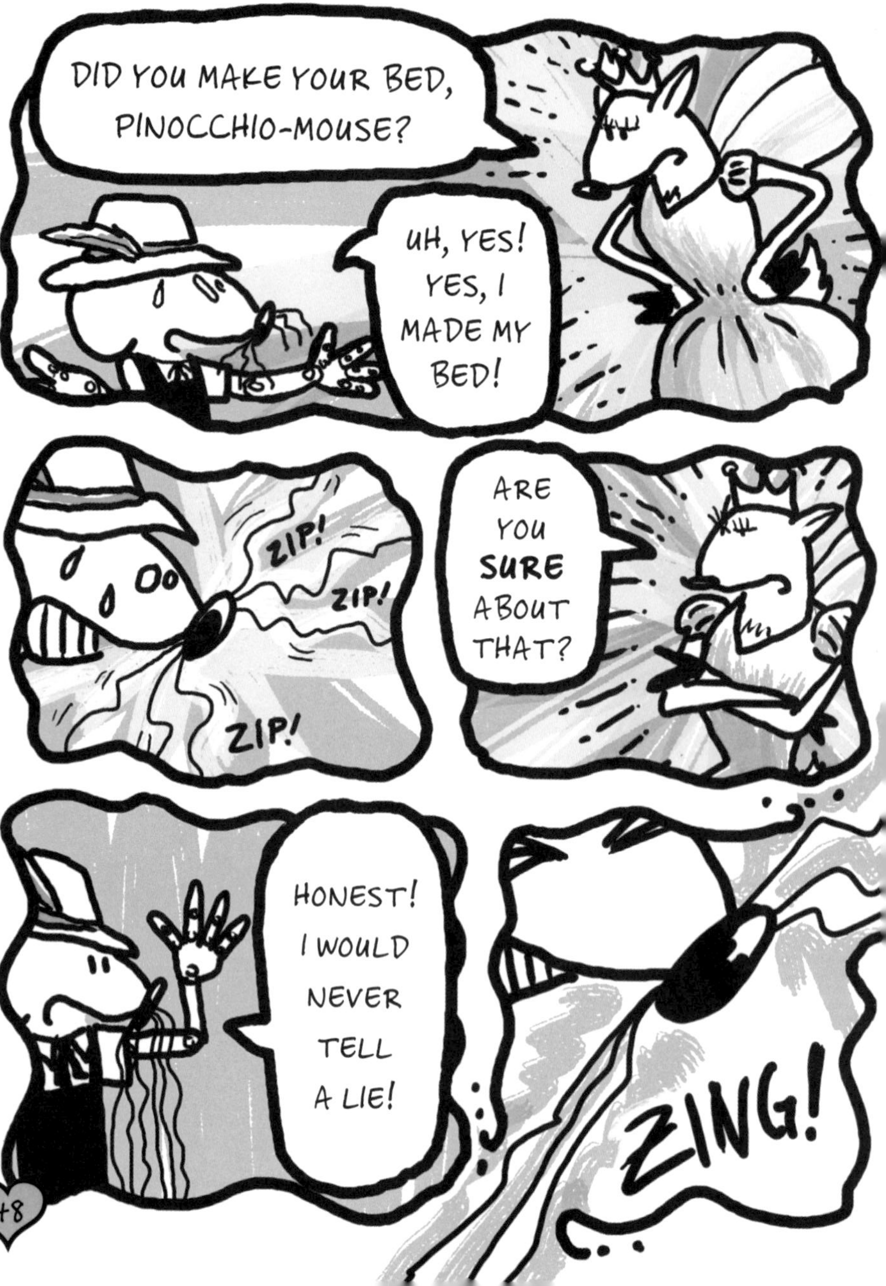
DID YOU MAKE YOUR BED, PINOCCHIO-MOUSE?
UH, YES! YES, I MADE MY BED!
ZIP!
ZIP!
ZIP!
ARE YOU **SURE** ABOUT THAT?
HONEST! I WOULD NEVER TELL A LIE!
ZING!

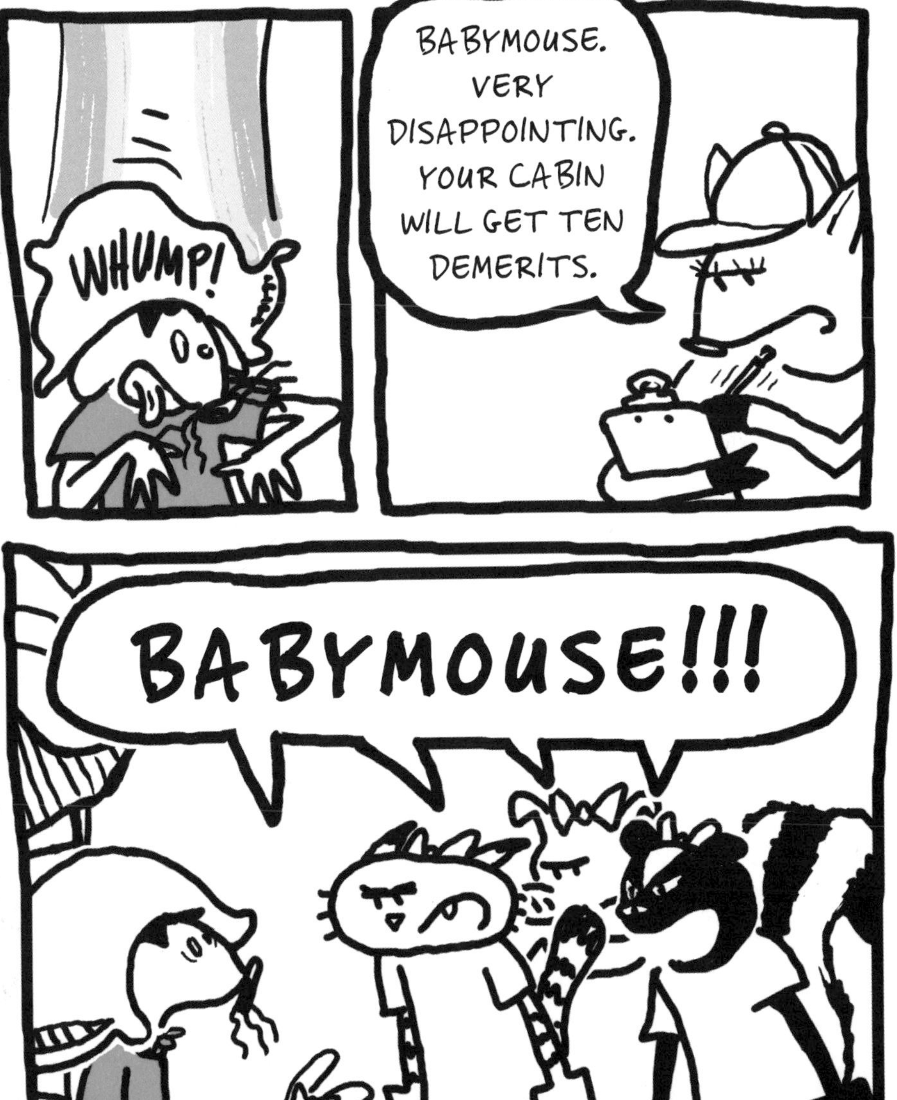
WHUMP!
BABYMOUSE. VERY DISAPPOINTING. YOUR CABIN WILL GET TEN DEMERITS.
BABYMOUSE!!!

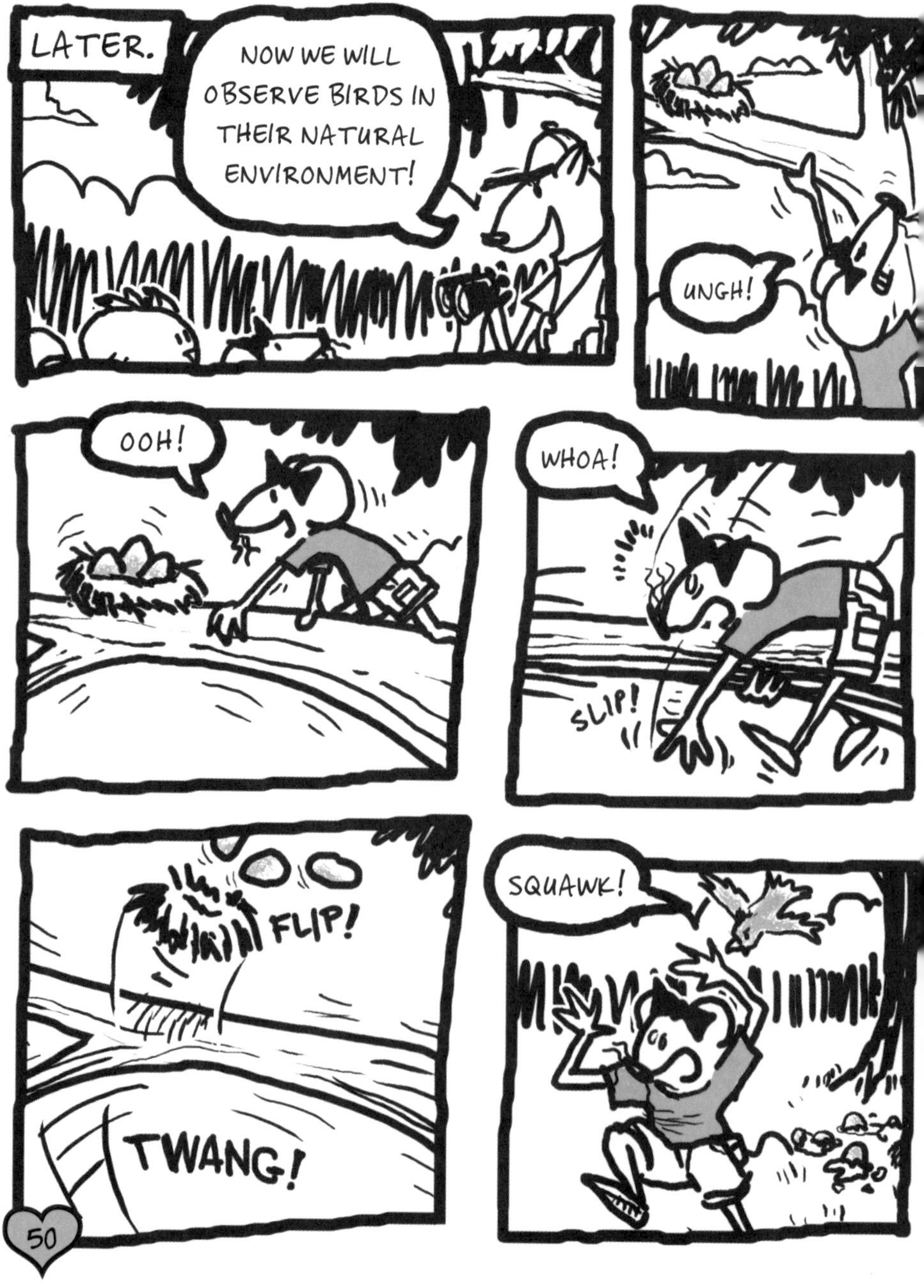
LATER.
NOW WE WILL OBSERVE BIRDS IN THEIR NATURAL ENVIRONMENT!
UNGH!
OOH!
WHOA!
SLIP!
FLIP!
TWANG!
SQUAWK!

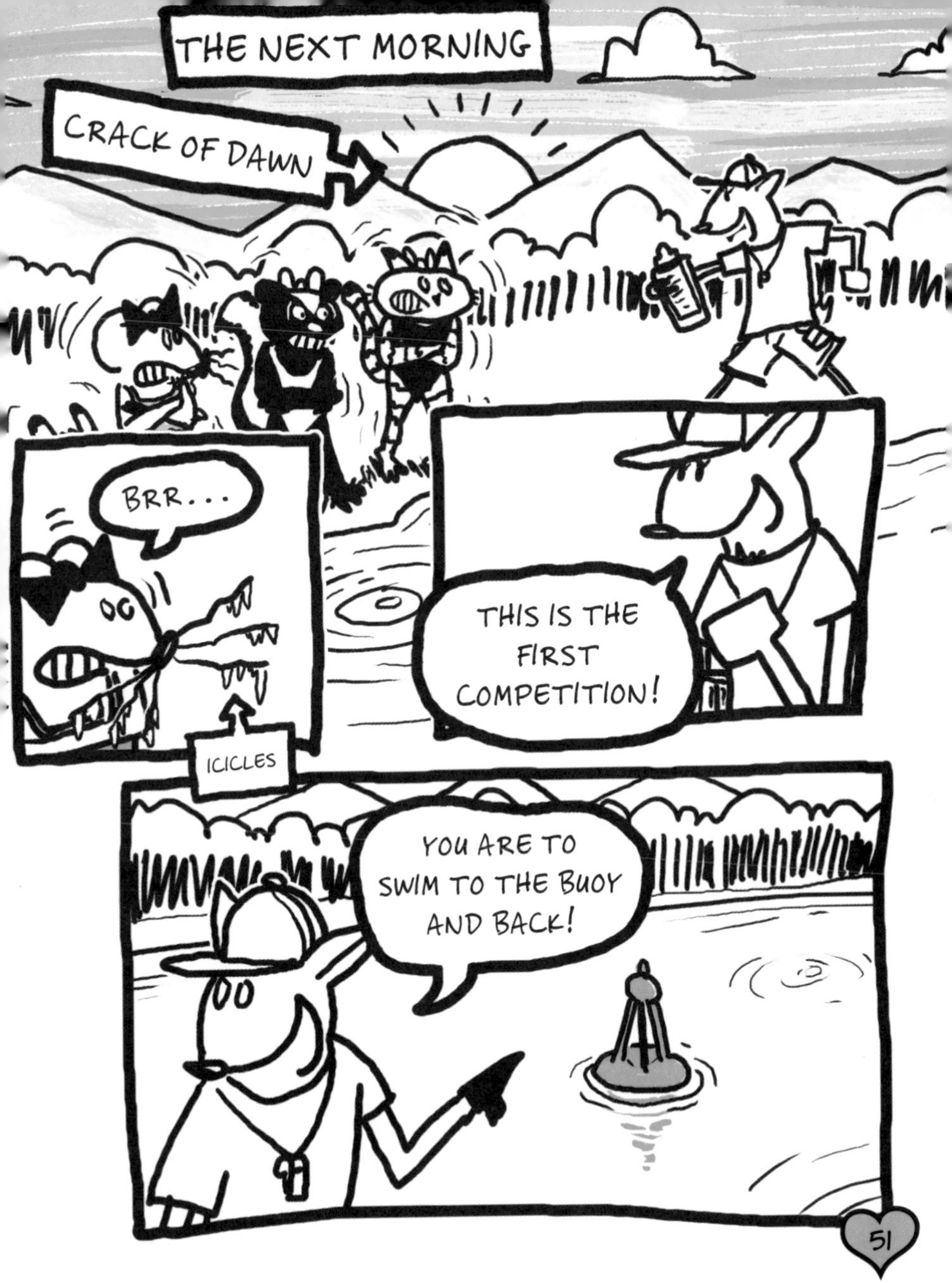
THE NEXT MORNING
CRACK OF DAWN
BRR...
ICICLES
THIS IS THE FIRST COMPETITION!
YOU ARE TO SWIM TO THE BUOY AND BACK!

BRR!
DIP
ON YOUR MARK, GET SET, GO!
TWEEET!
SPLASH!
SPLASH!
SPLASH!
SPLASH!

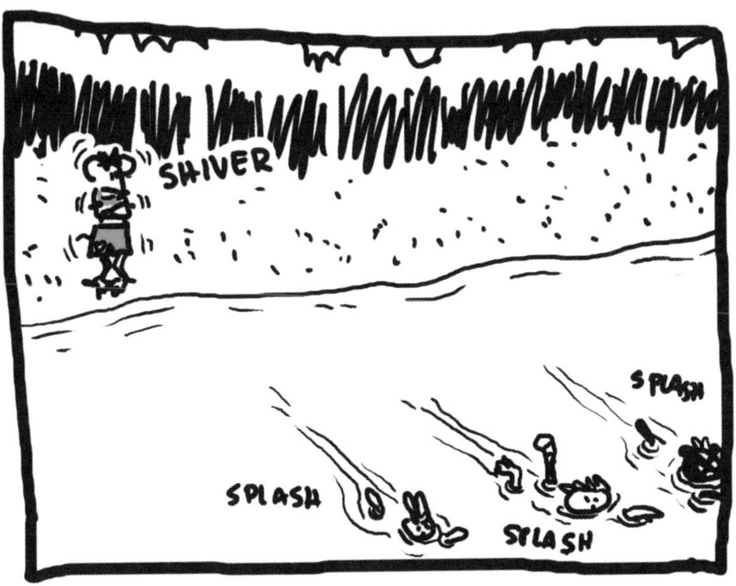
SHIVER
SPLASH
SPLASH
SPLASH
SPLASH

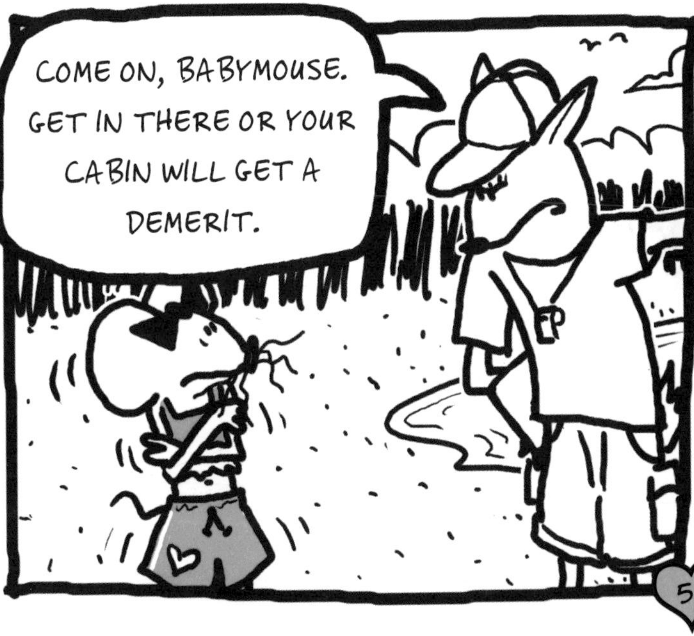
COME ON, BABYMOUSE. GET IN THERE OR YOUR CABIN WILL GET A DEMERIT.

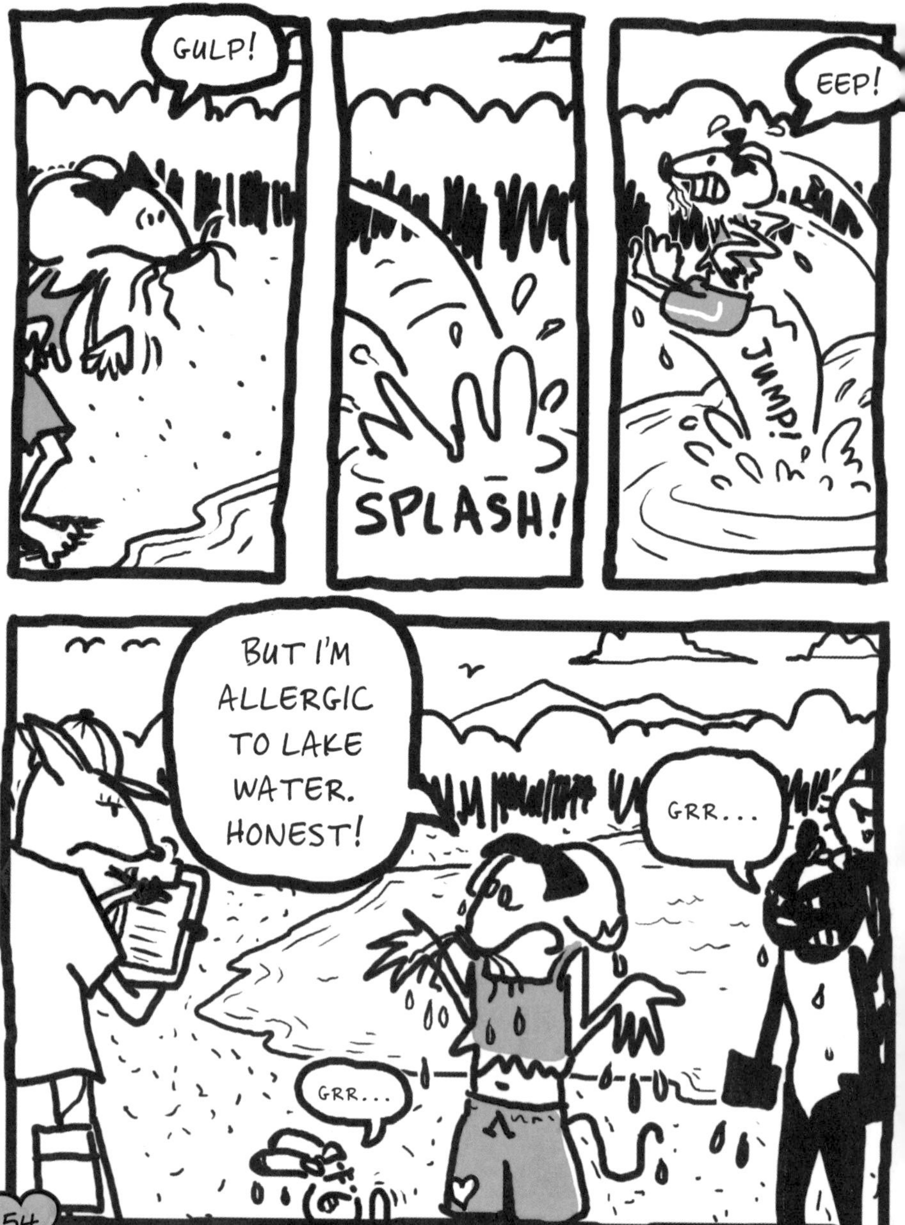
GULP!
SPLASH!
EEP!
JUMP!
BUT I'M ALLERGIC TO LAKE WATER. HONEST!
GRR...
GRR...

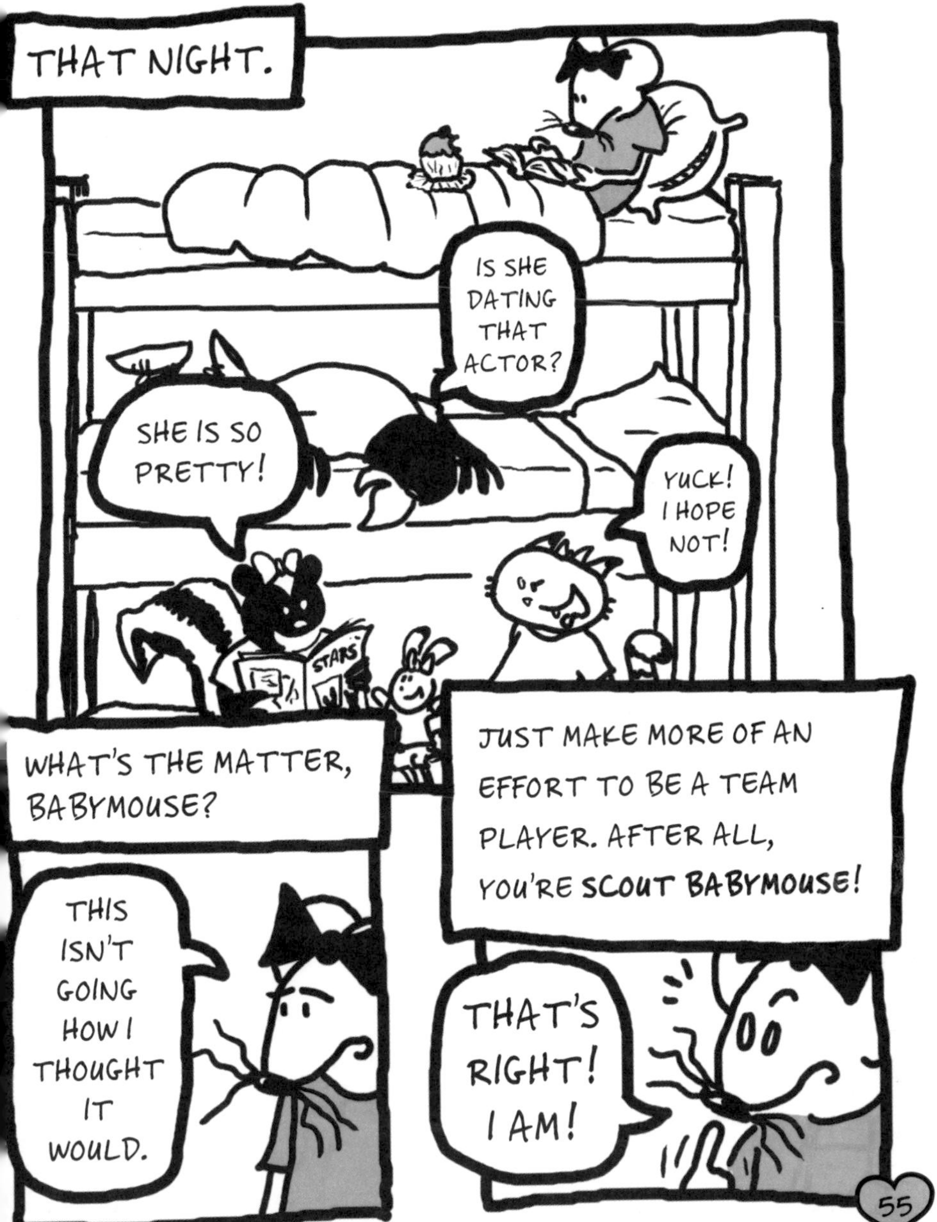
THAT NIGHT.
IS SHE DATING THAT ACTOR?
SHE IS SO PRETTY!
YUCK! I HOPE NOT!
STARS
WHAT'S THE MATTER, BABYMOUSE?
THIS ISN'T GOING HOW I THOUGHT IT WOULD.
JUST MAKE MORE OF AN EFFORT TO BE A TEAM PLAYER. AFTER ALL, YOU'RE **SCOUT BABYMOUSE**!
THAT'S RIGHT! I AM!

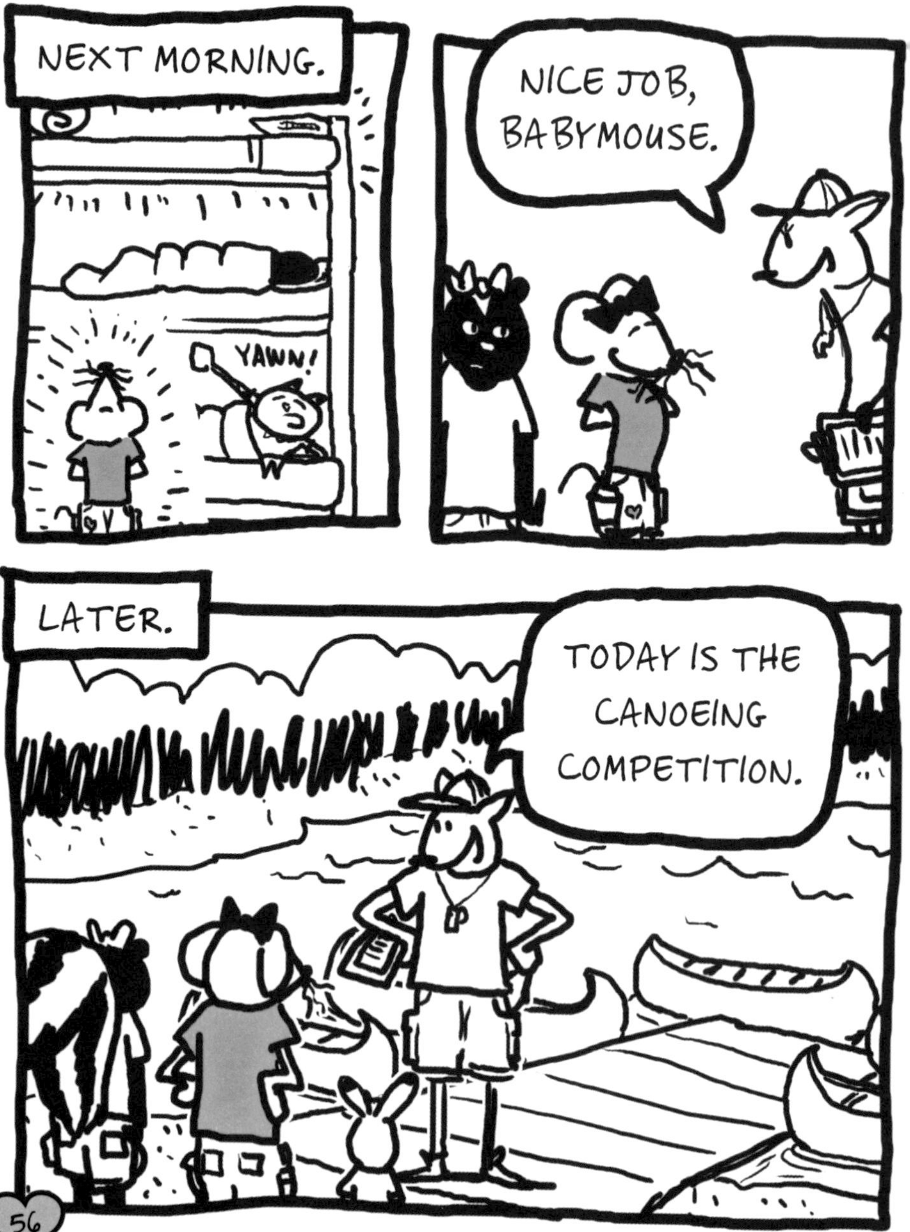
NEXT MORNING.
YAWN!
NICE JOB, BABYMOUSE.
LATER.
TODAY IS THE CANOEING COMPETITION.

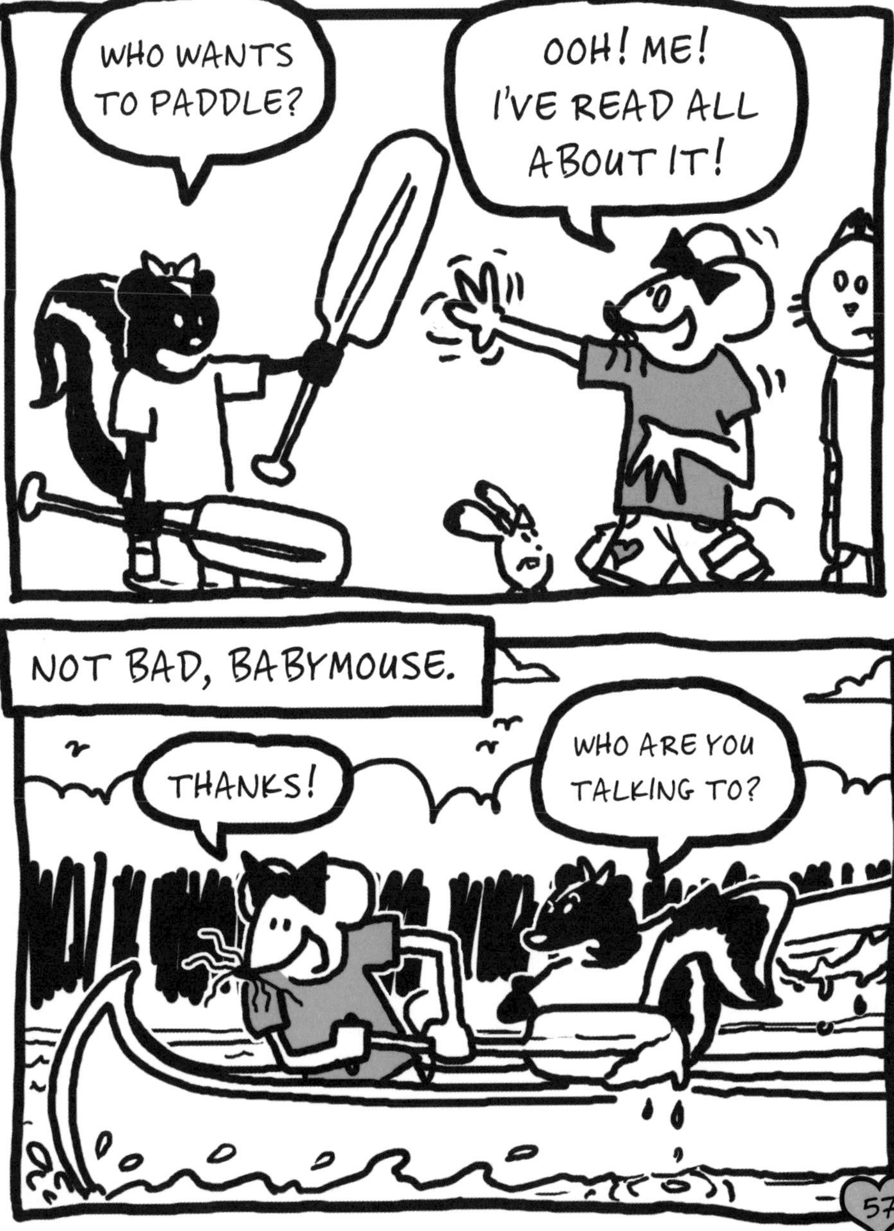
WHO WANTS TO PADDLE?
OOH! ME! I'VE READ ALL ABOUT IT!
NOT BAD, BABYMOUSE.
THANKS!
WHO ARE YOU TALKING TO?

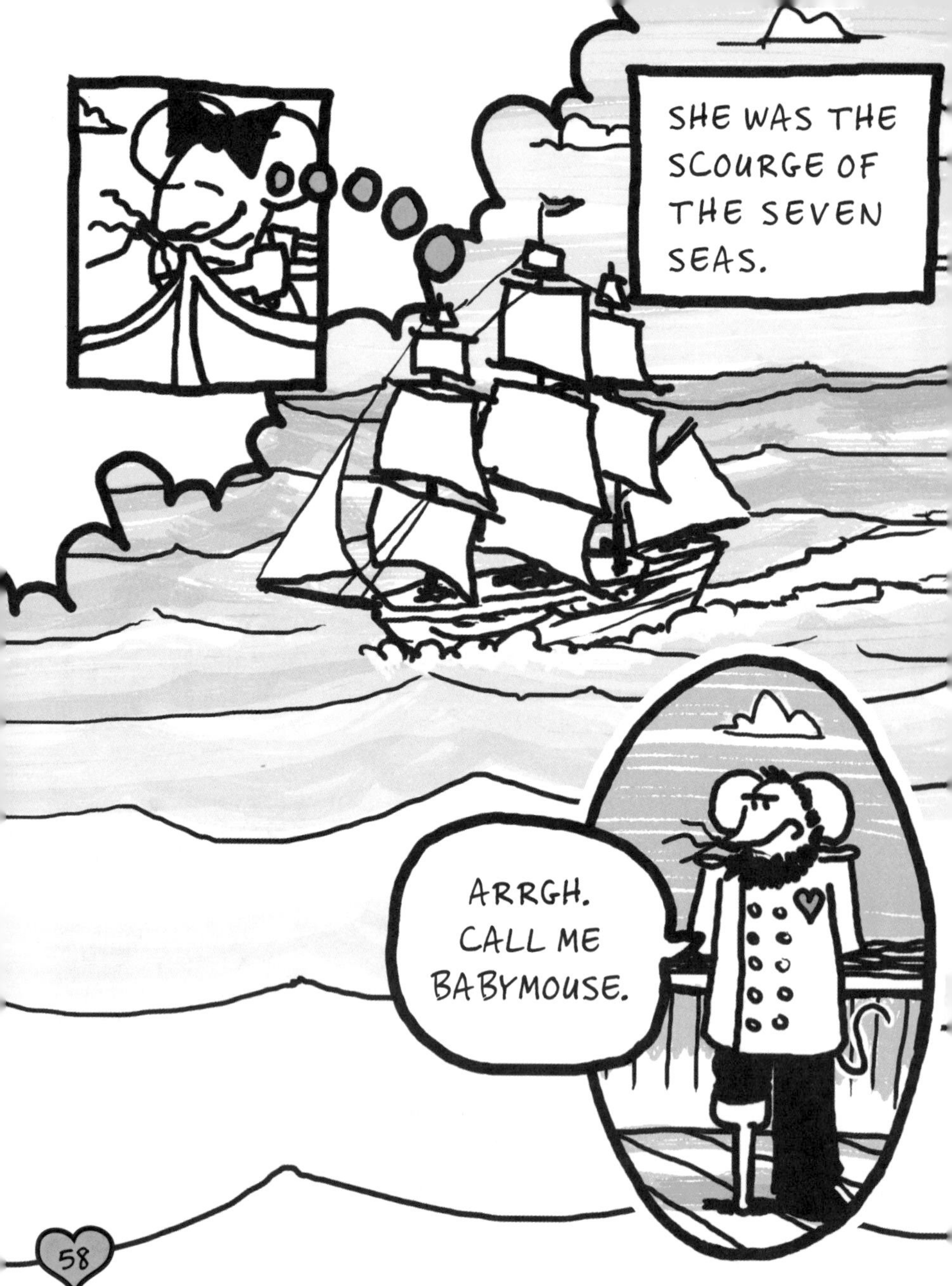
SHE WAS THE SCOURGE OF THE SEVEN SEAS.
ARRGH. CALL ME BABYMOUSE.

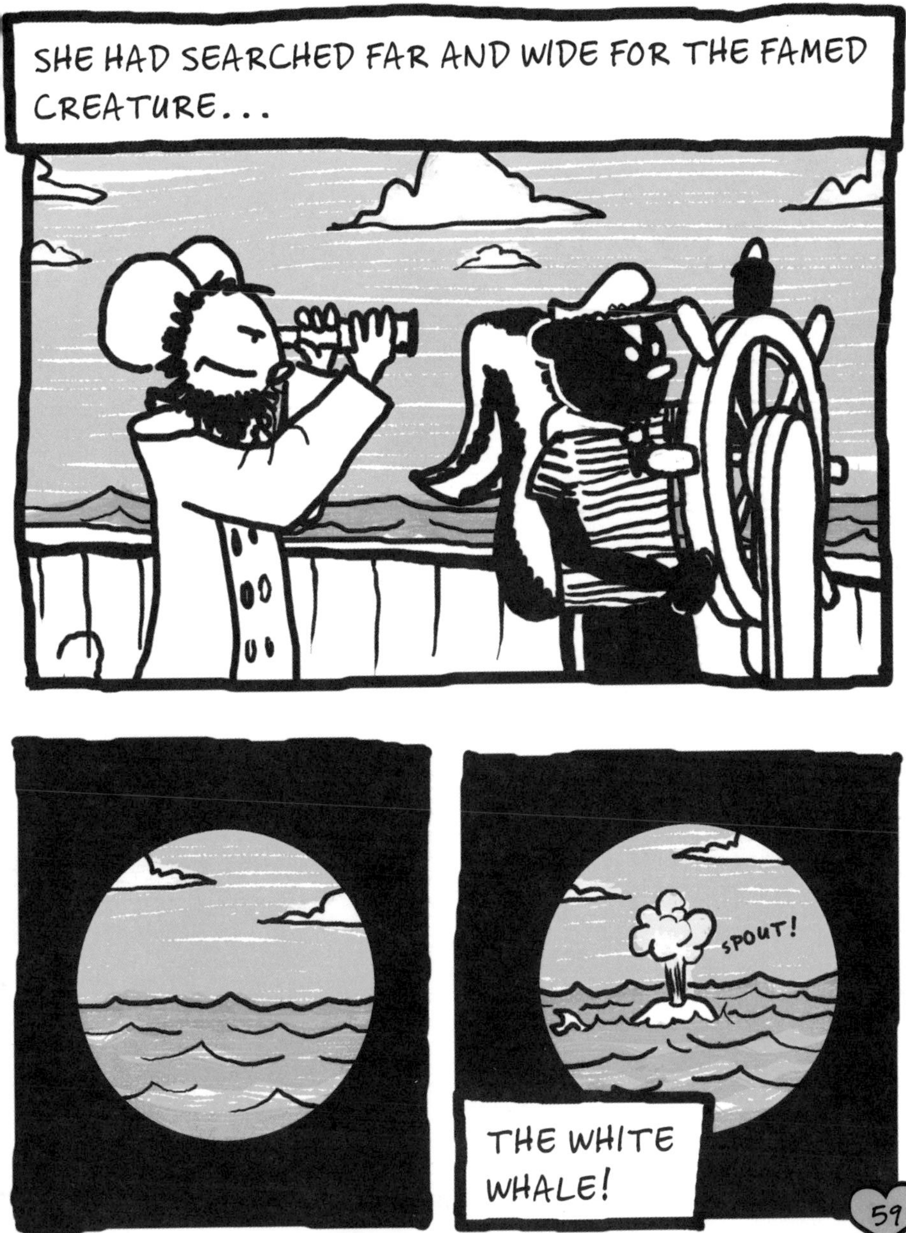
SHE HAD SEARCHED FAR AND WIDE FOR THE FAMED CREATURE...
SPOUT!
THE WHITE WHALE!

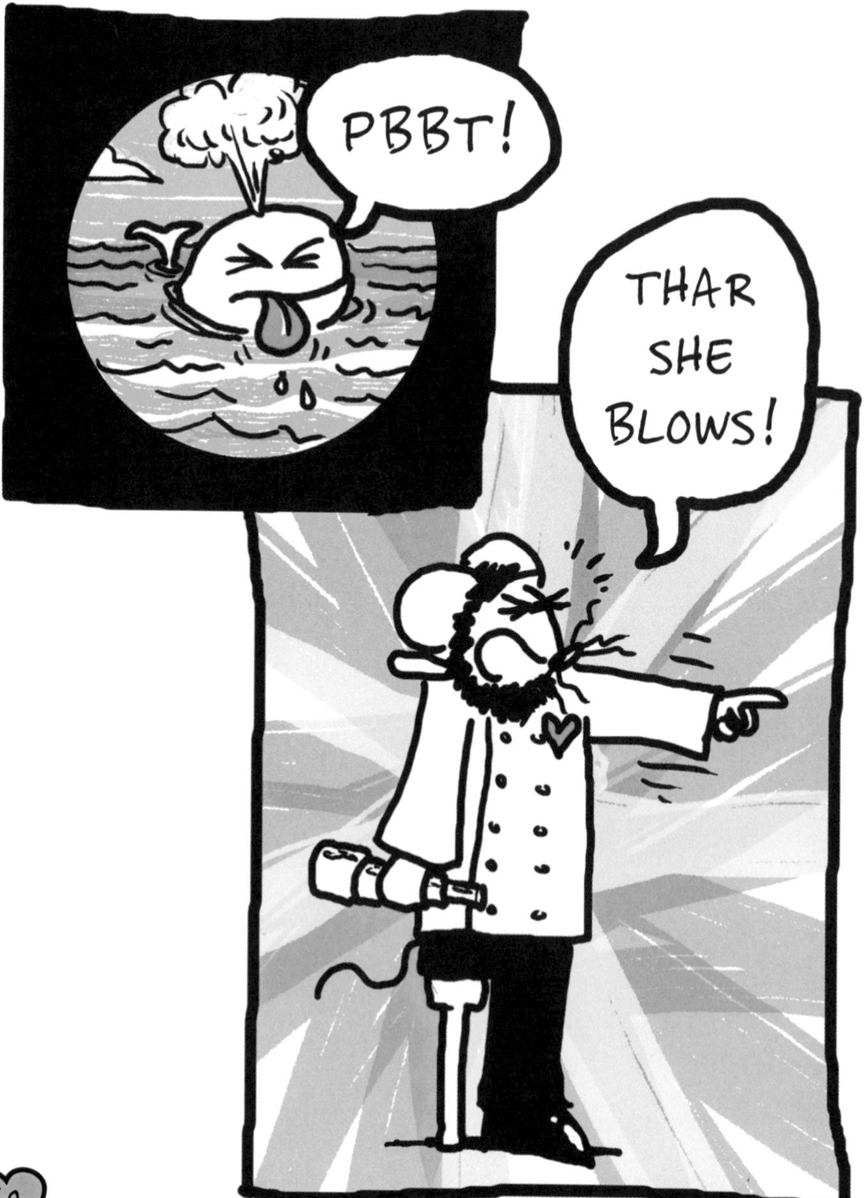
PBBT!
THAR SHE BLOWS!

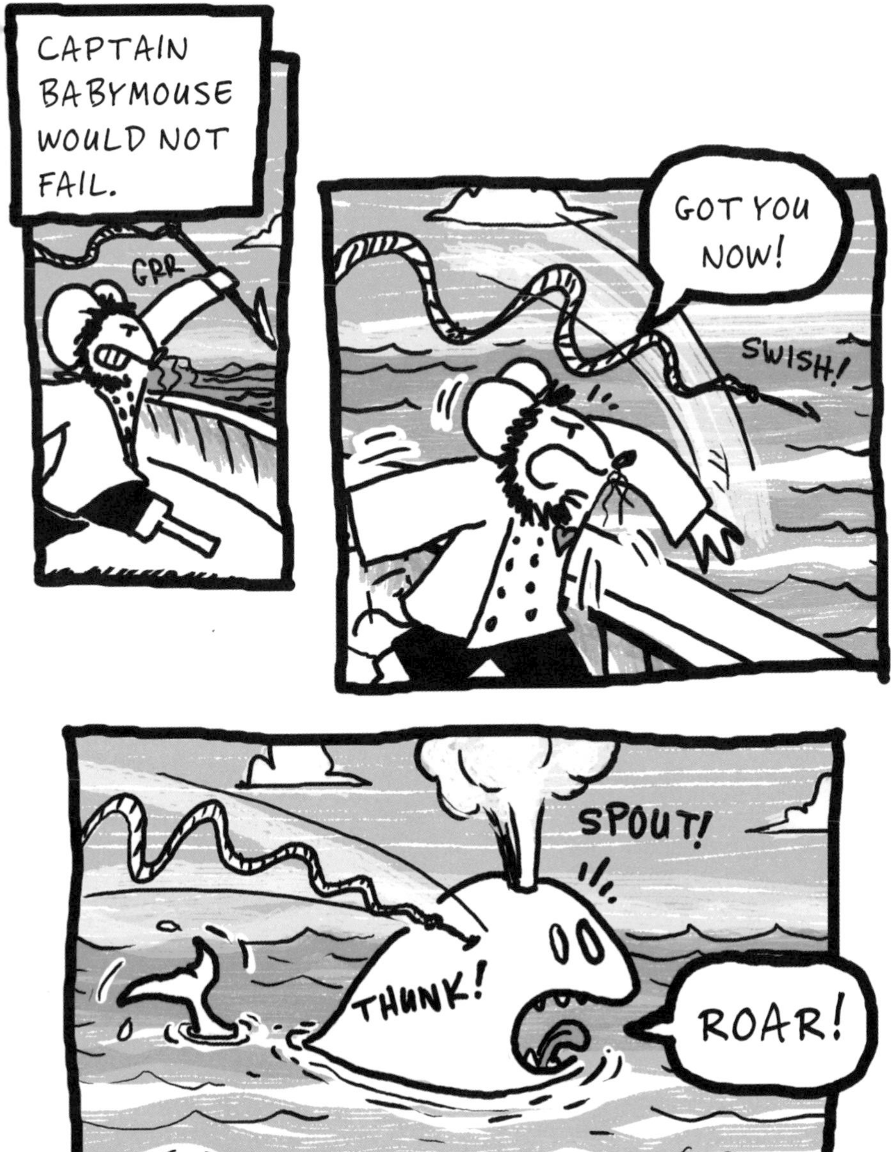
CAPTAIN BABYMOUSE WOULD NOT FAIL.
GRR
GOT YOU NOW!
SWISH!
SPOUT!
THUNK!
ROAR!

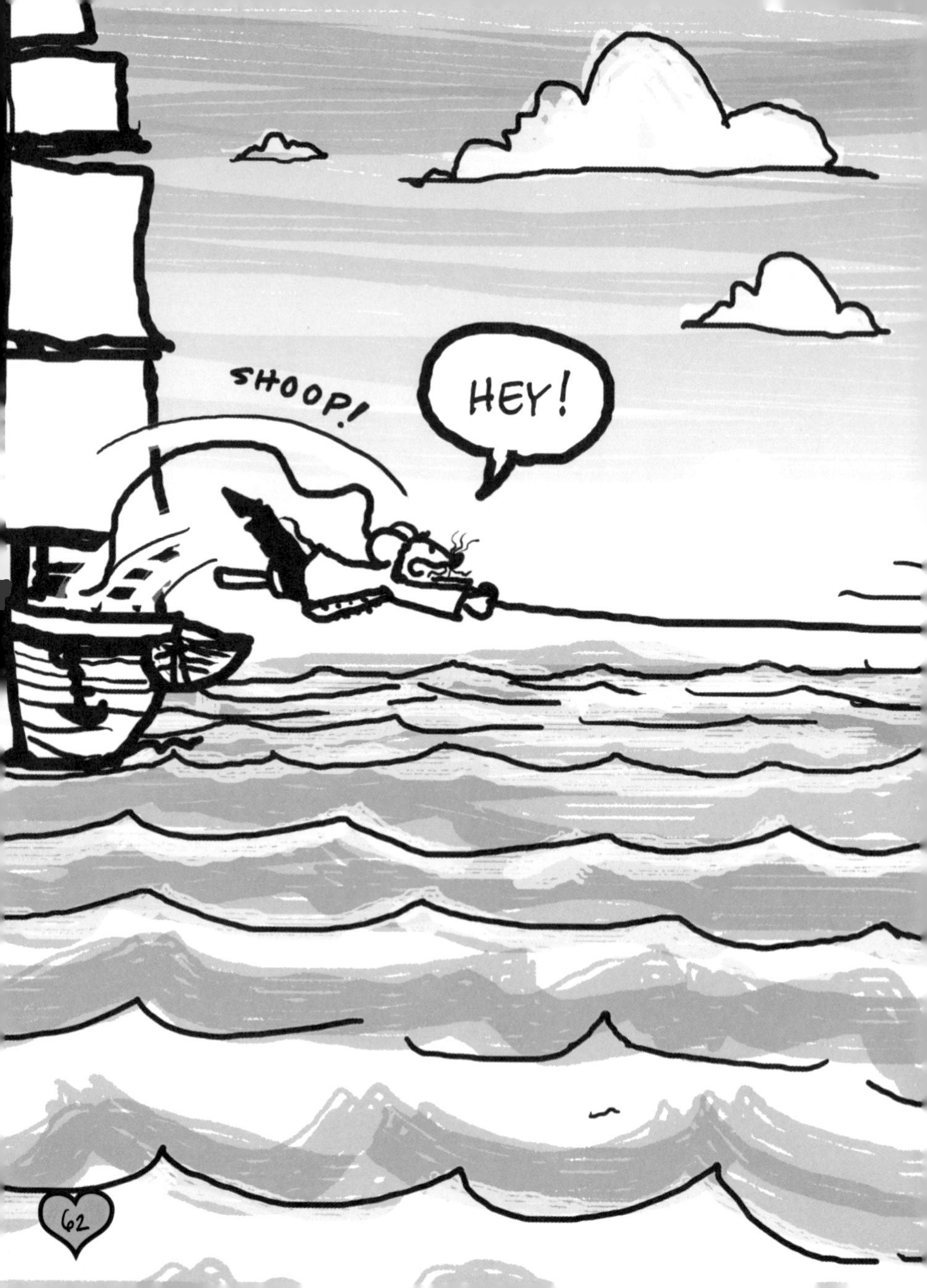
SHOOP!
HEY!

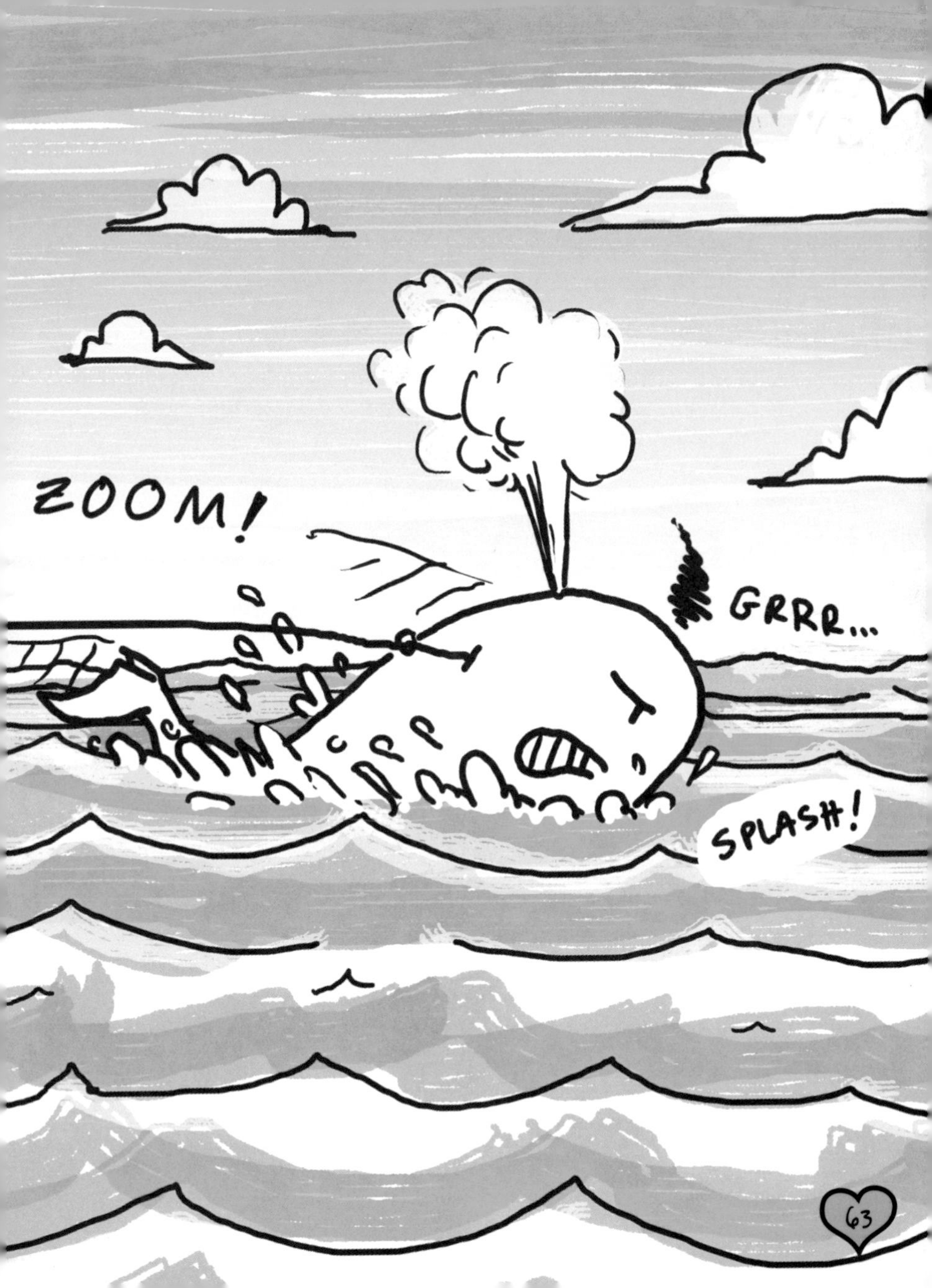
ZOOM!
GRRR...
SPLASH!

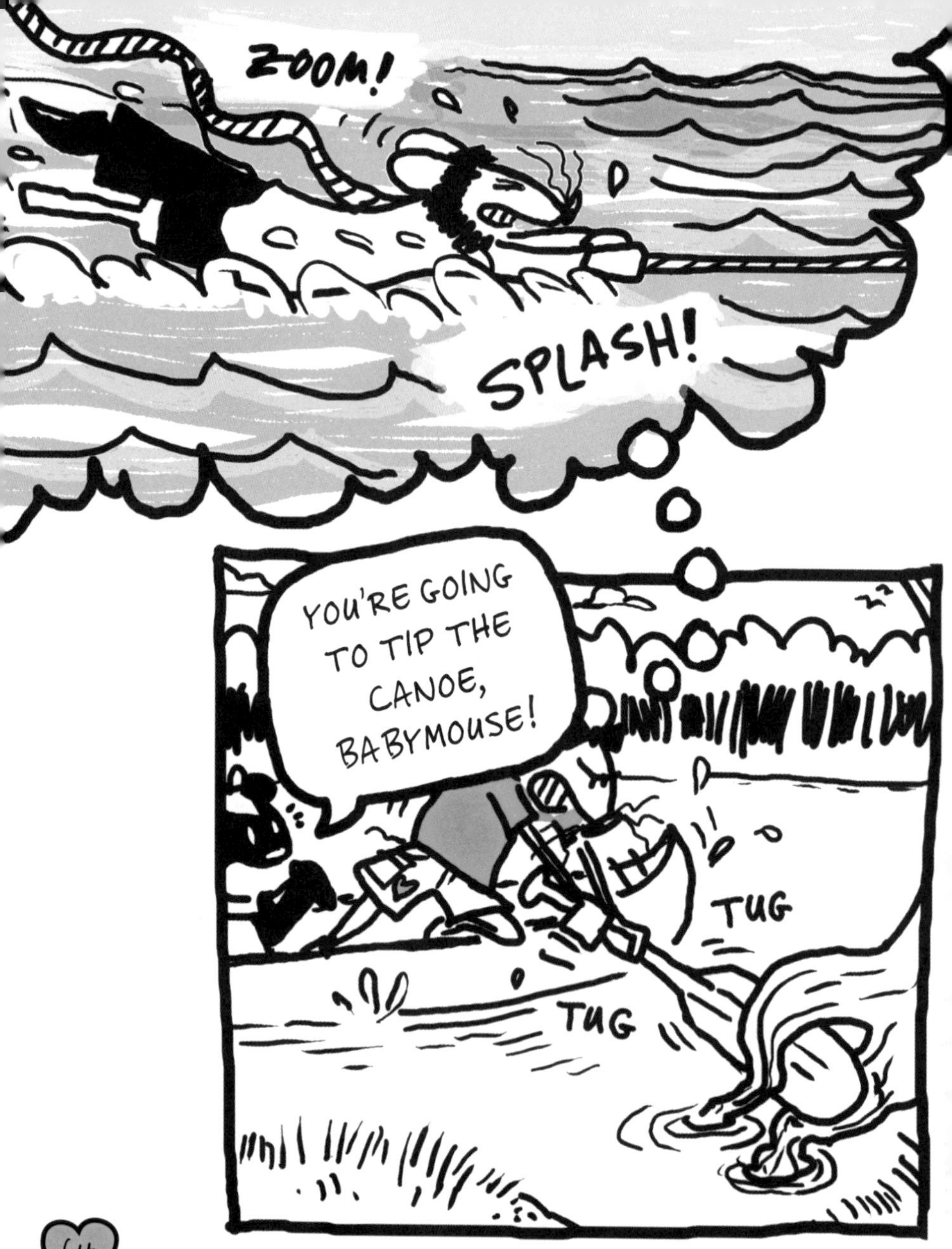
ZOOM!
SPLASH!
YOU'RE GOING TO TIP THE CANOE, BABYMOUSE!
TUG
TUG

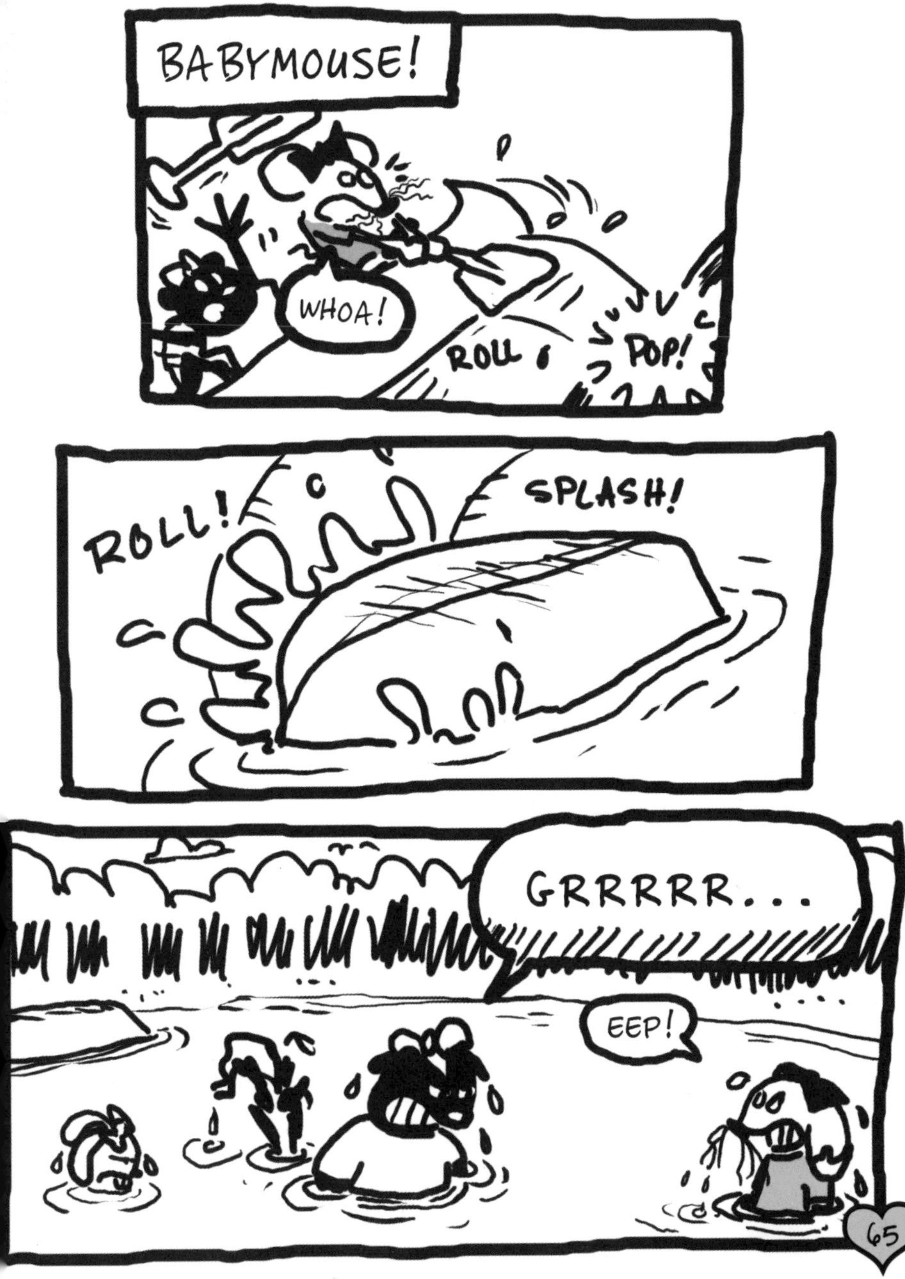
BABYMOUSE!
WHOA!
ROLL
POP!
ROLL!
SPLASH!
GRRRRR...
EEP!

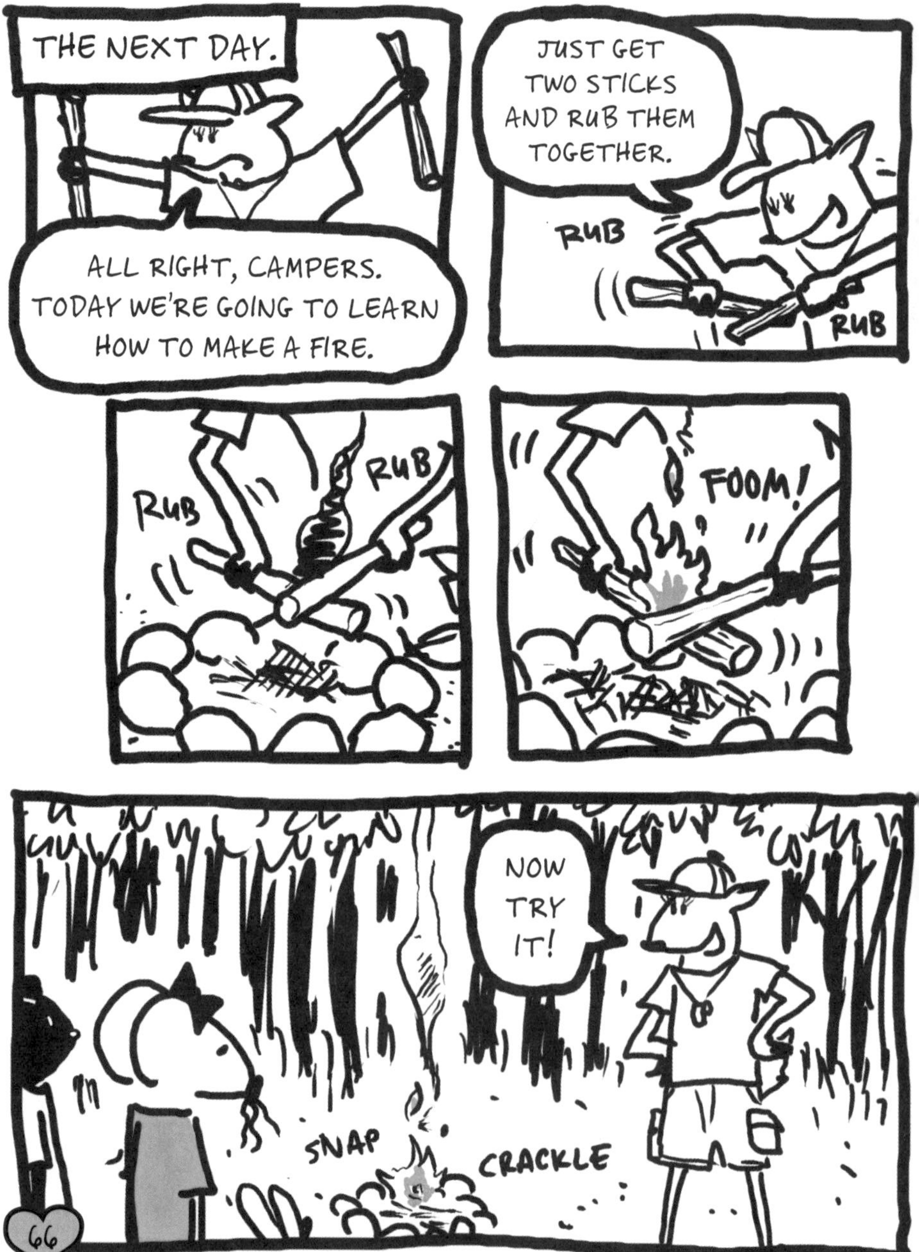
THE NEXT DAY.
ALL RIGHT, CAMPERS. TODAY WE'RE GOING TO LEARN HOW TO MAKE A FIRE.
JUST GET TWO STICKS AND RUB THEM TOGETHER.
RUB
RUB
RUB
RUB
FOOM!
NOW TRY IT!
SNAP
CRACKLE

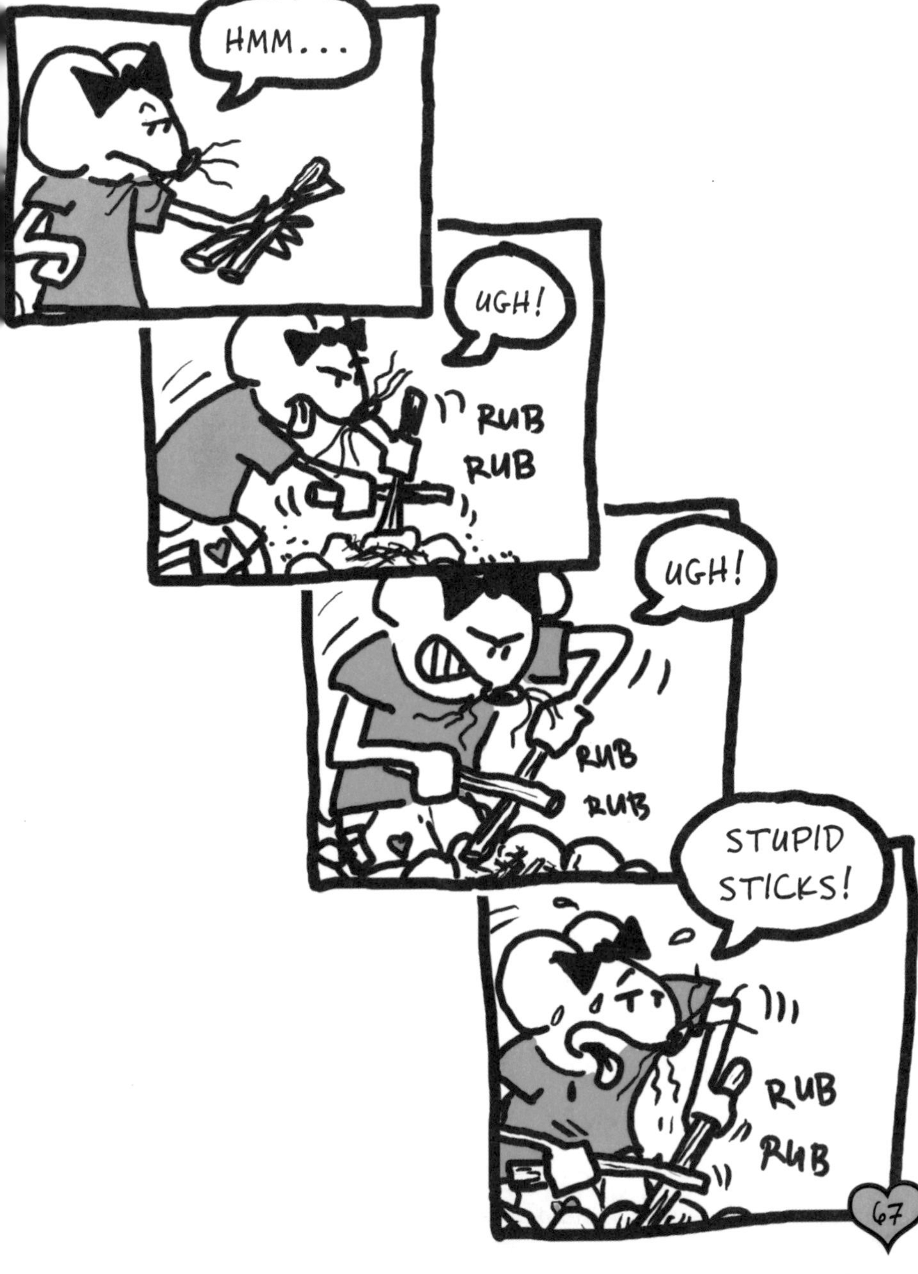
HMM...
UGH!
RUB
RUB
UGH!
RUB
RUB
STUPID STICKS!
RUB
RUB

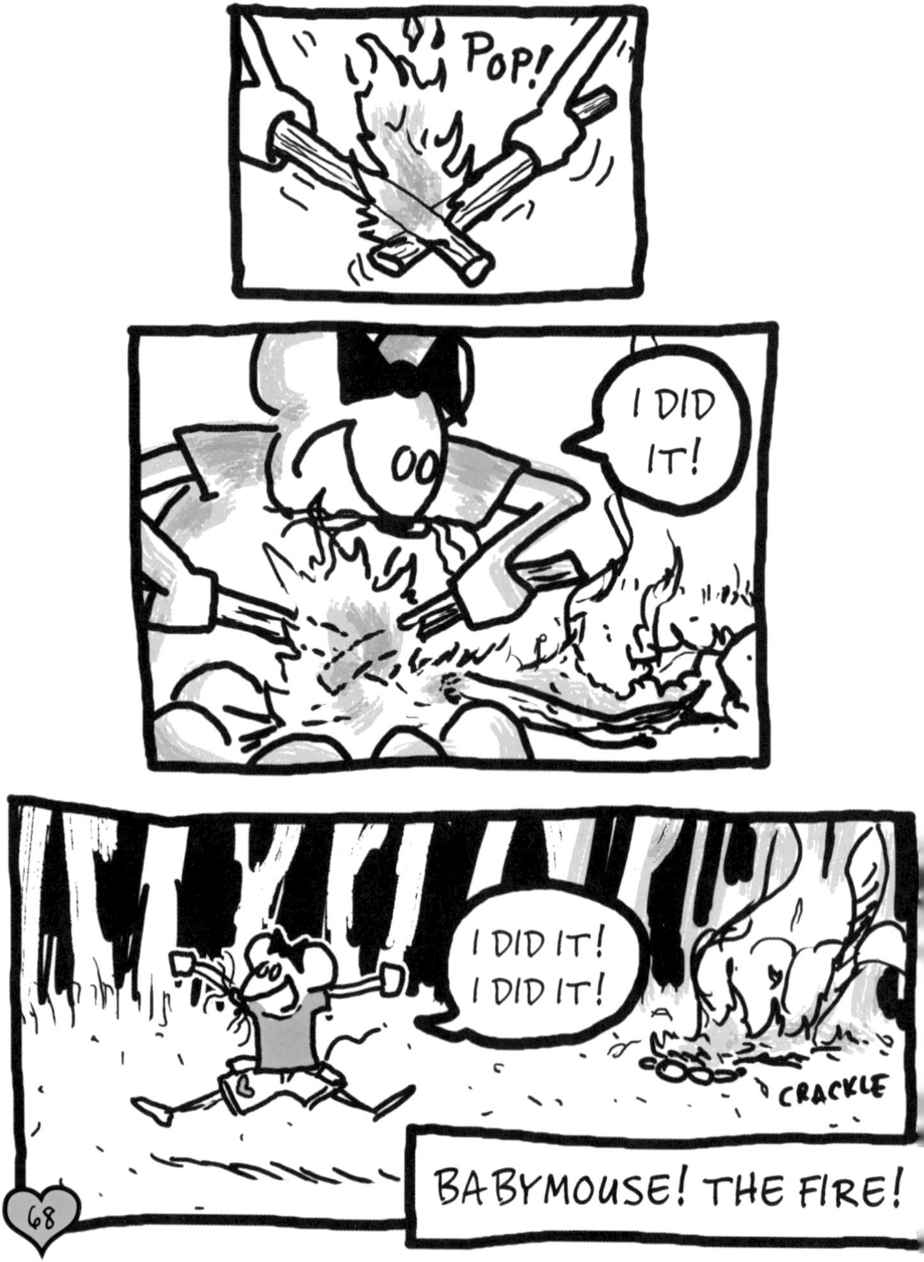
POP!
I DID IT!
I DID IT! I DID IT!
CRACKLE
BABYMOUSE! THE FIRE!

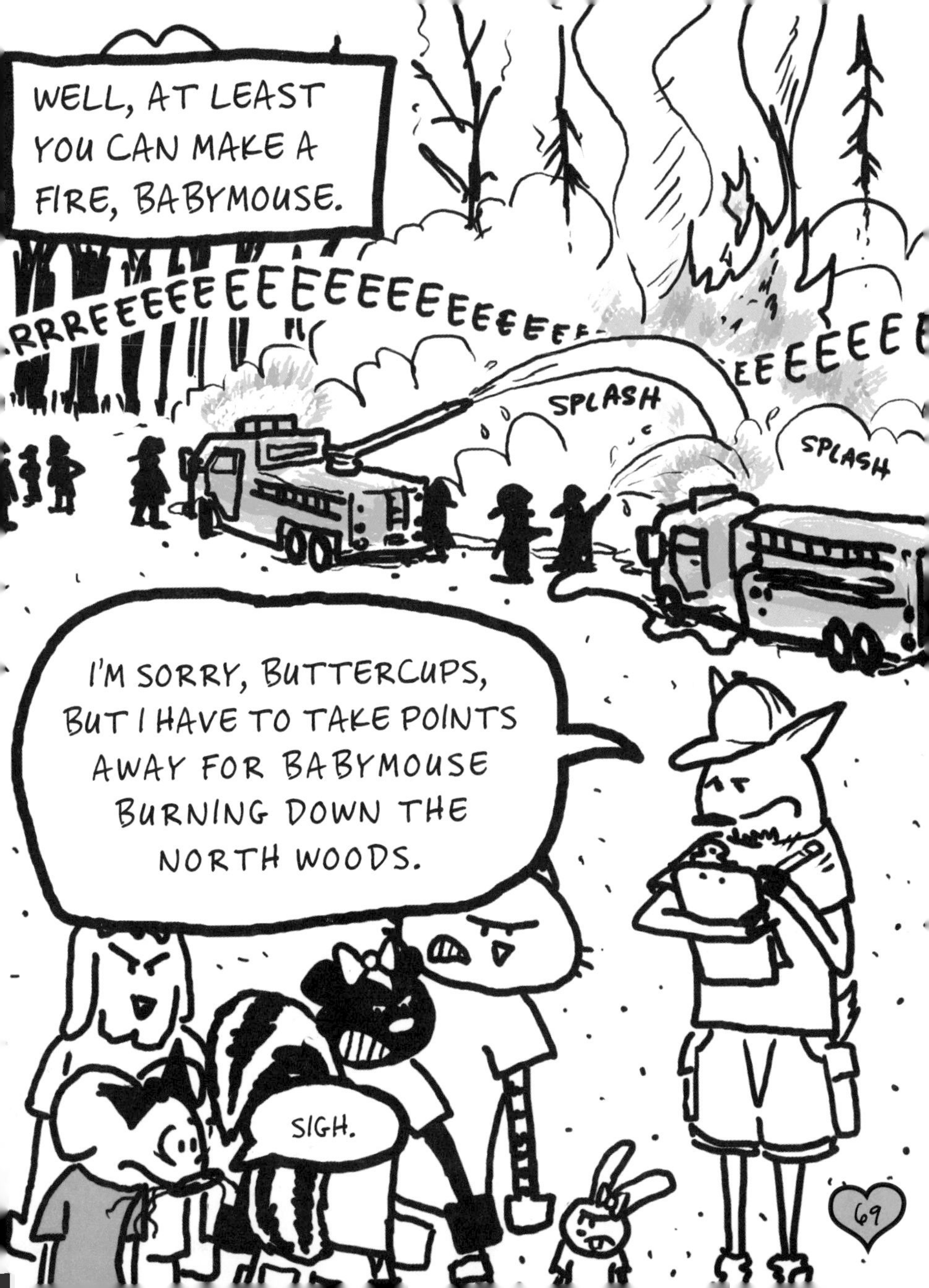

WELL, AT LEAST YOU CAN MAKE A FIRE, BABYMOUSE.
RRREEEEEEEEEEEEEEEEEEE
EEEEEEEE
SPLASH
SPLASH
I'M SORRY, BUTTERCUPS, BUT I HAVE TO TAKE POINTS AWAY FOR BABYMOUSE BURNING DOWN THE NORTH WOODS.
SIGH.

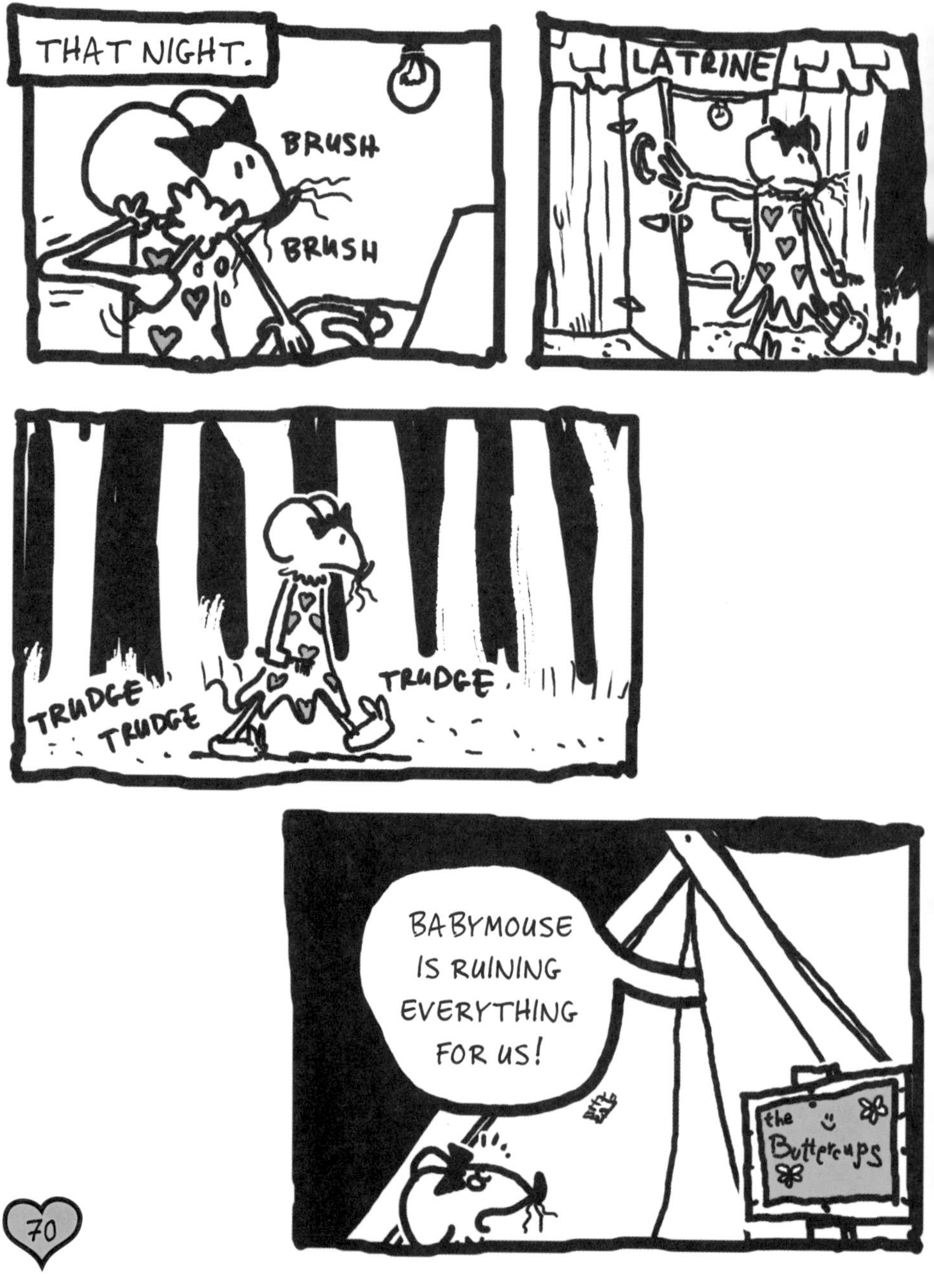
THAT NIGHT.
BRUSH
BRUSH
LATRINE
TRUDGE
TRUDGE
TRUDGE
BABYMOUSE IS RUINING EVERYTHING FOR US!
the Buttercups

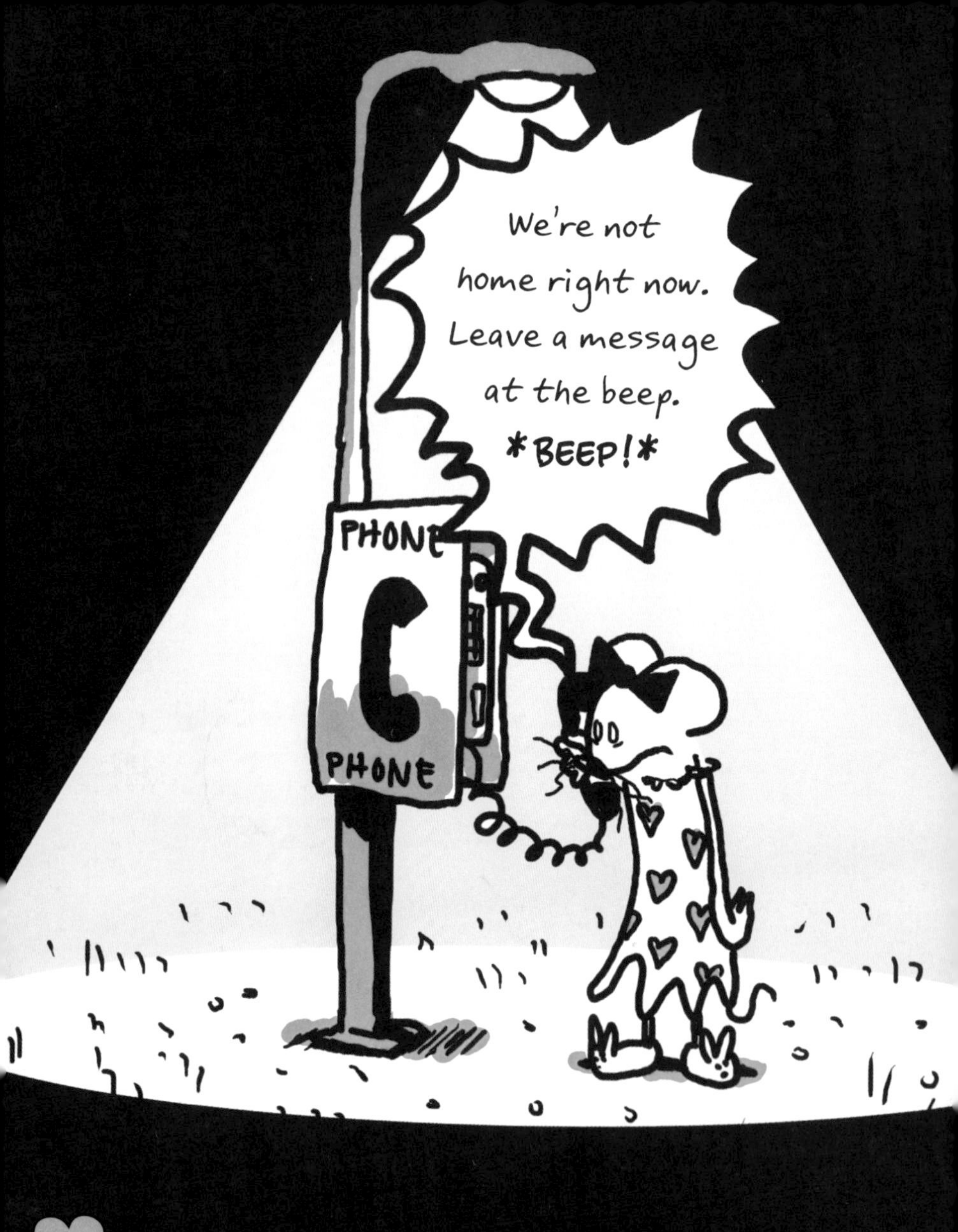
We're not home right now. Leave a message at the beep. *BEEP!*
PHONE
PHONE

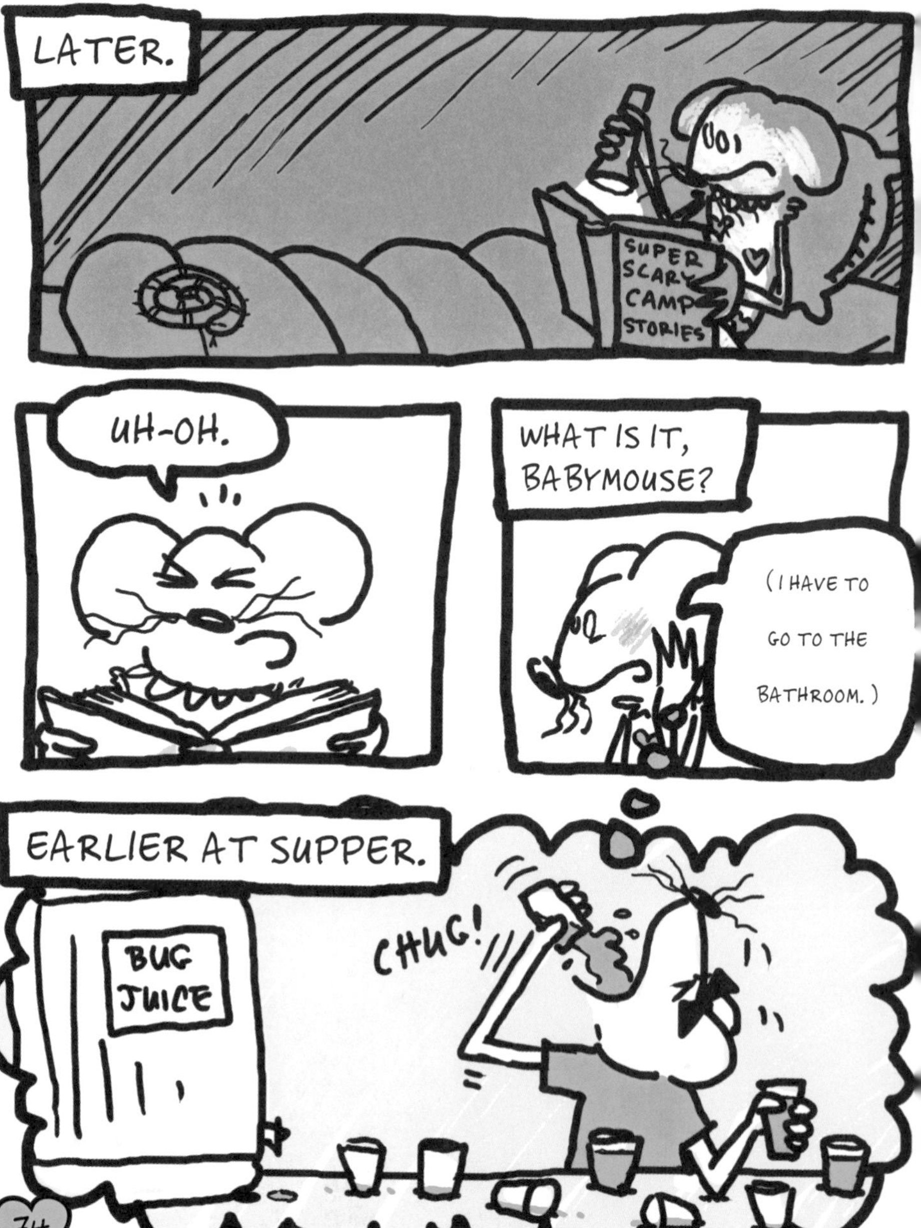
LATER.
SUPER SCARY CAMP STORIES
UH-OH.
WHAT IS IT, BABYMOUSE?
(I HAVE TO GO TO THE BATHROOM.)
EARLIER AT SUPPER.
BUG JUICE
CHUG!

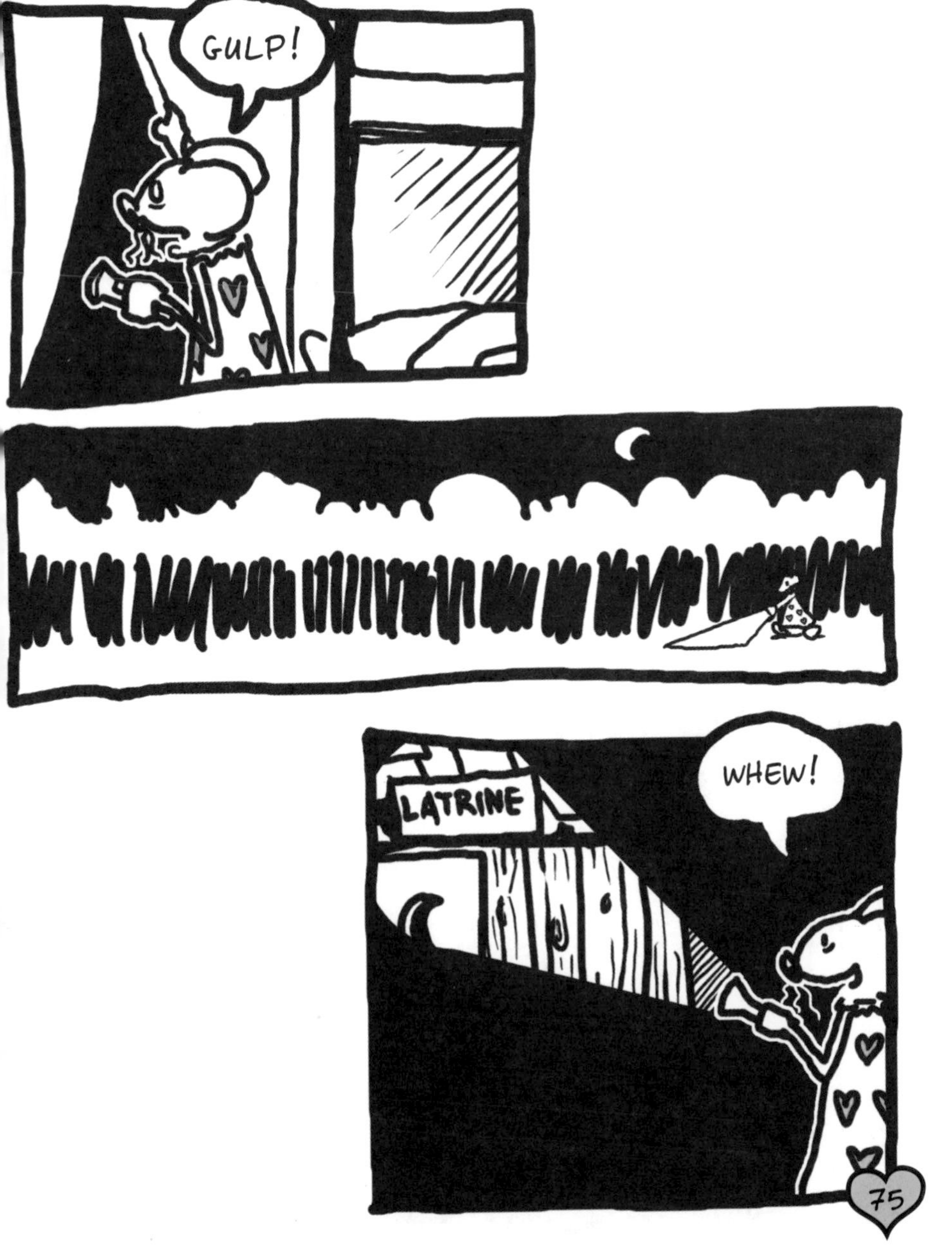
GULP!
LATRINE
WHEW!
75

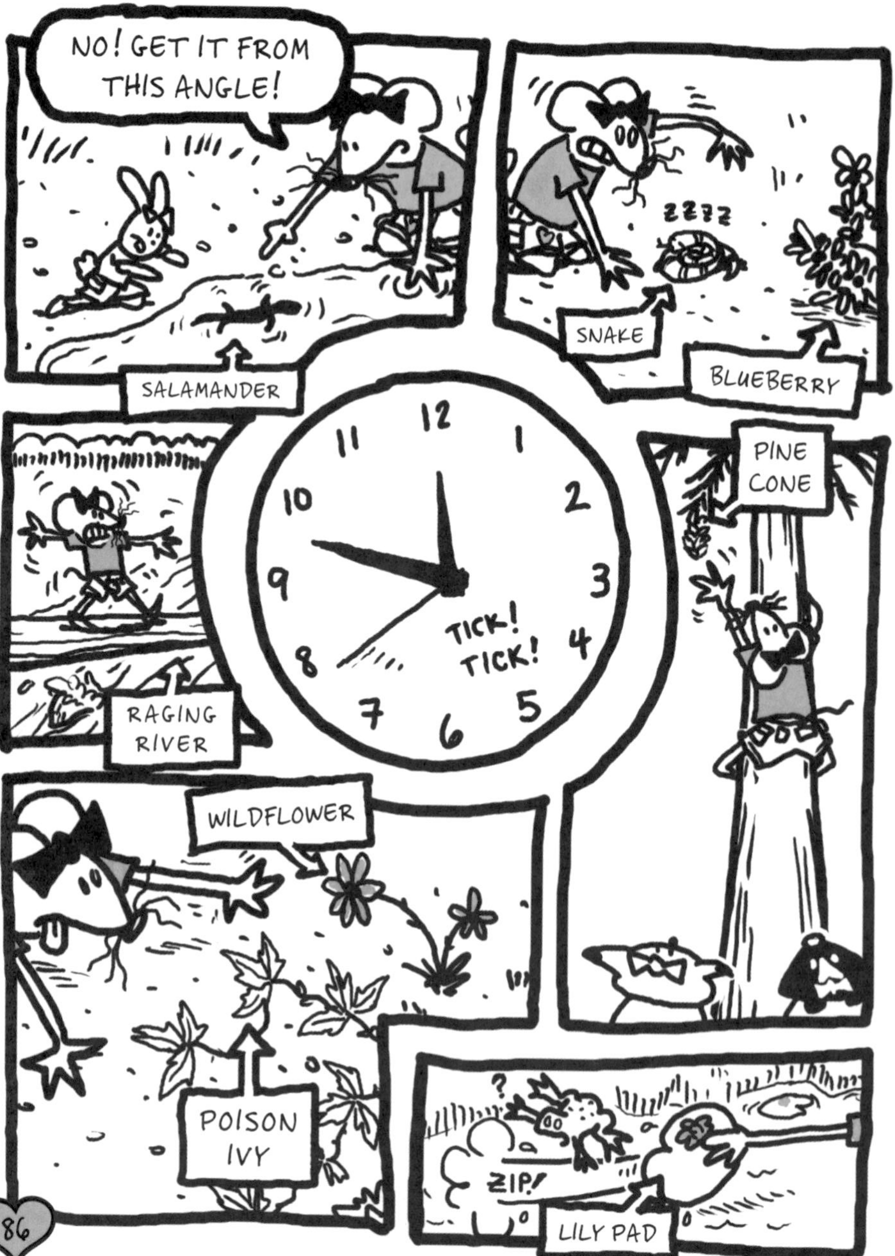

NO! GET IT FROM THIS ANGLE!
SALAMANDER
ZZZZ
SNAKE
BLUEBERRY
12 1 2 3 4 5 6 7 8 9 10 11
TICK! TICK!
PINE CONE
RAGING RIVER
WILDFLOWER
POISON IVY
?
ZIP!
LILY PAD

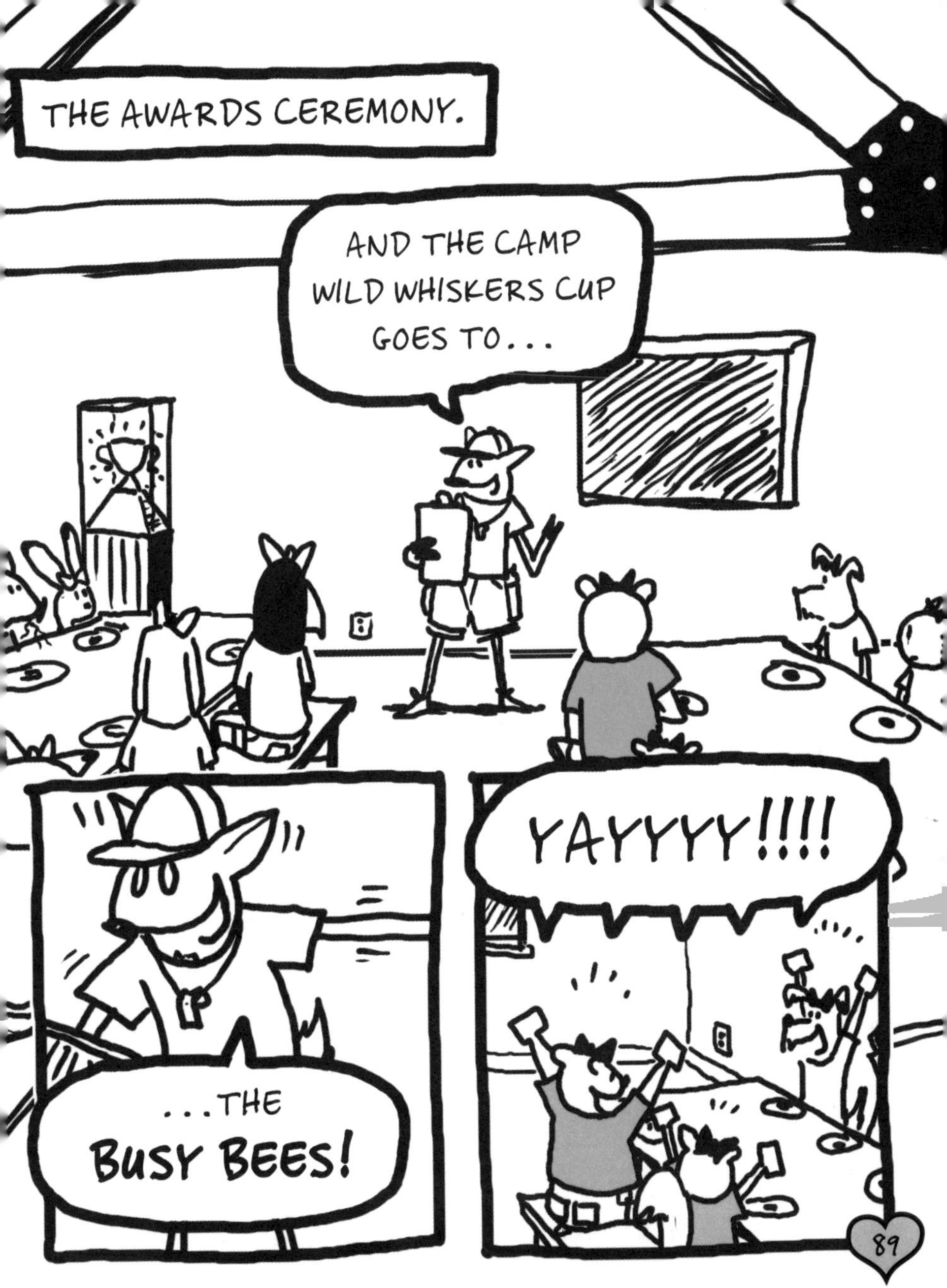
THE AWARDS CEREMONY.
AND THE CAMP WILD WHISKERS CUP GOES TO . . .
. . . THE BUSY BEES!
YAYYYYY!!!!

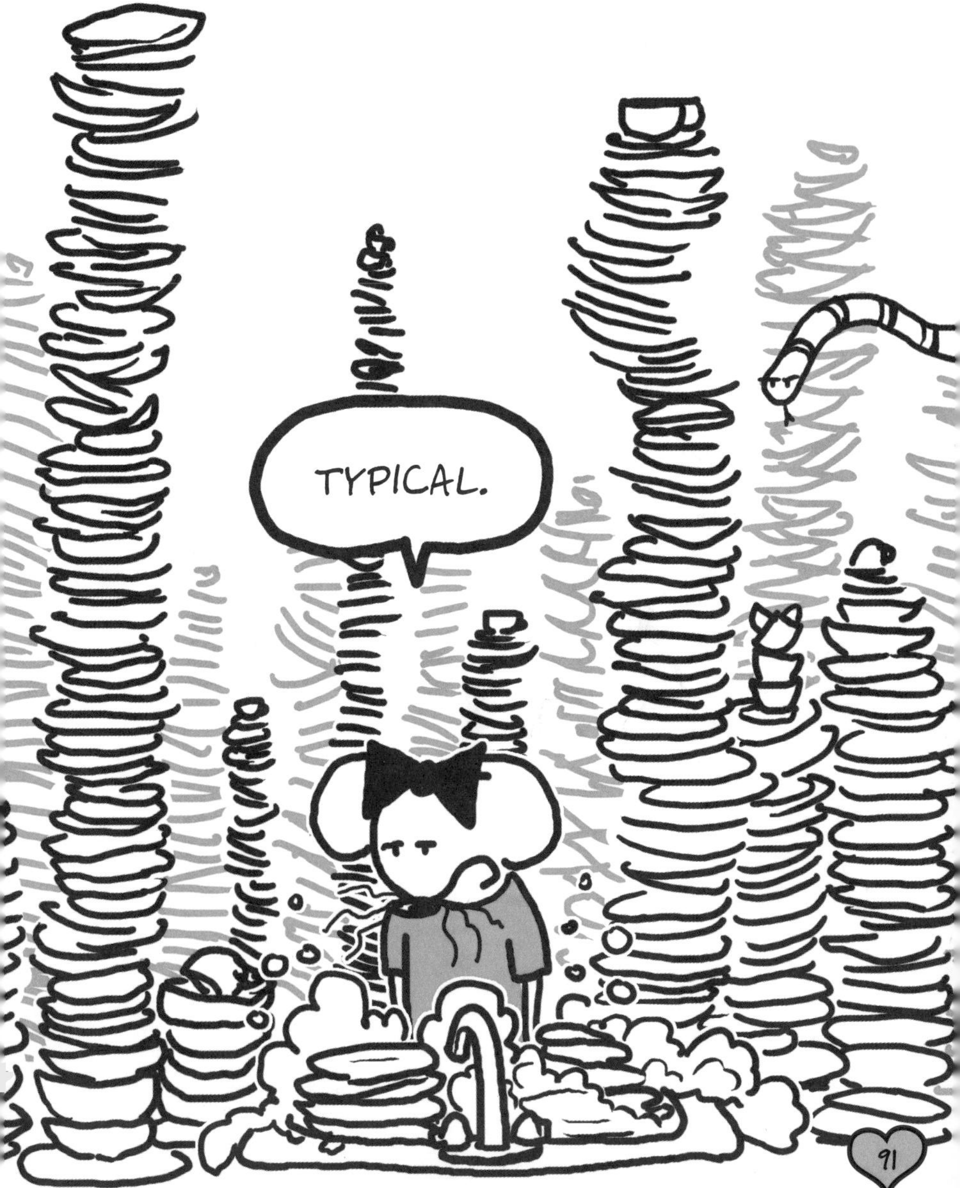
TYPICAL.

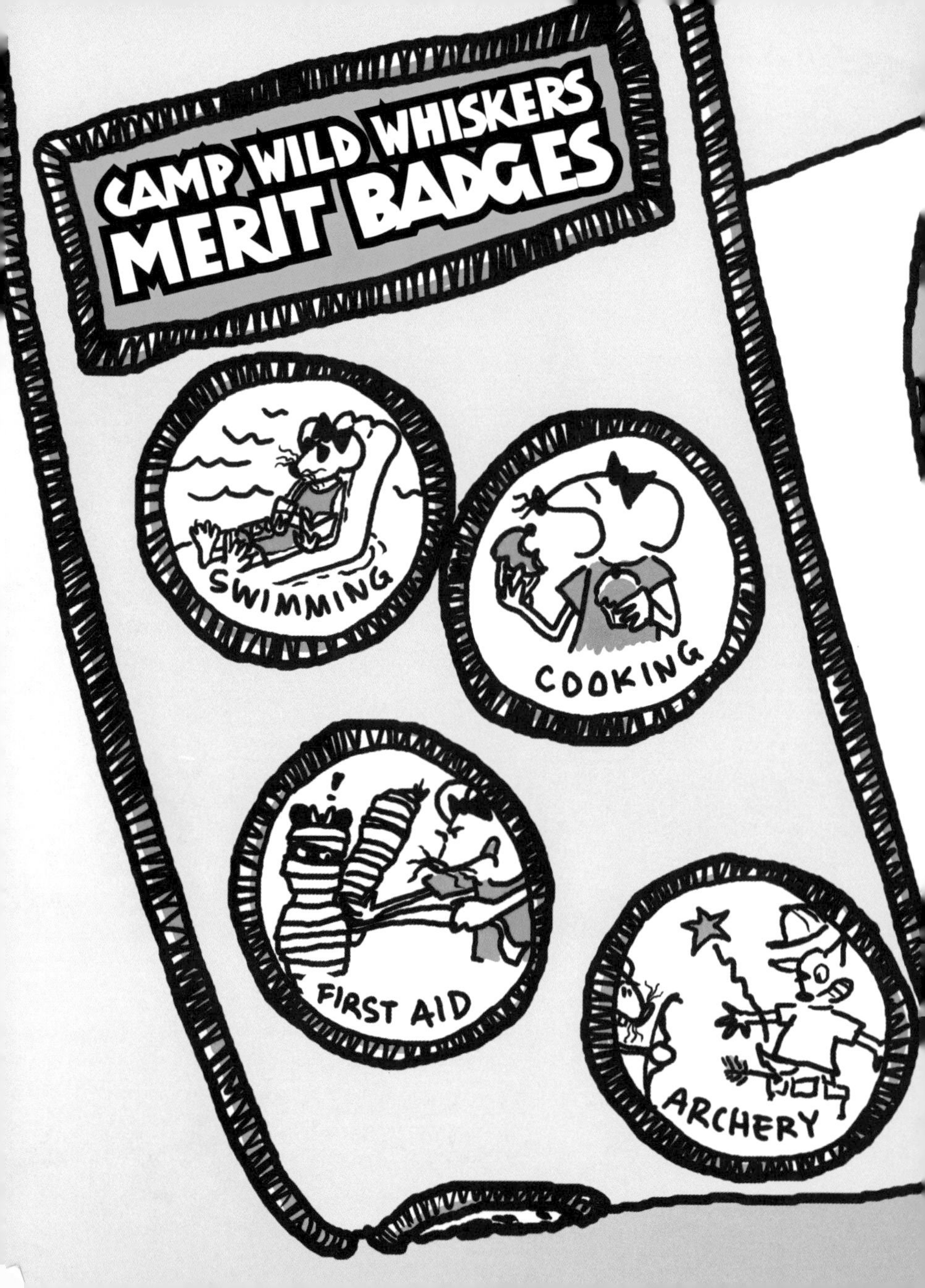
CAMP WILD WHISKERS
MERIT BADGES
SWIMMING
COOKING
FIRST AID
ARCHERY

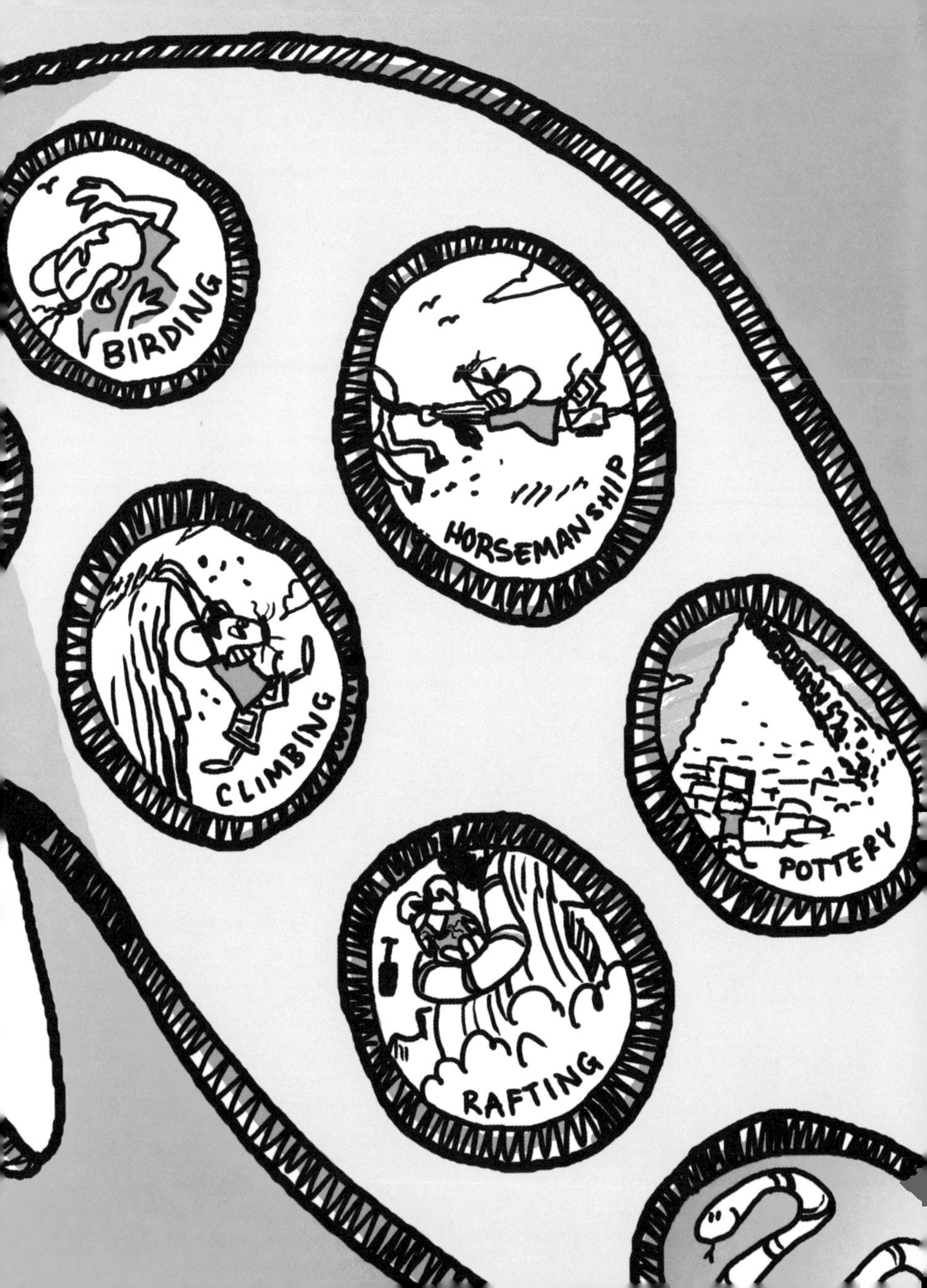
BIRDING
HORSEMANSHIP
CLIMBING
POTTERY
RAFTING